Final Silence

Ronald Flores

Translated by Gavin O'Toole

Aflame Books
2 The Green
Laverstock
Wiltshire
SP1 1QS
United Kingdom
email: info@aflamebooks.com

ISBN:9780955233920

First published in Spanish in 2001 as *Último silencio*
by Magna Terra/Bancafé, Guatemala

Copyright © Ronald Flores 2008
This English translation Copyright © Gavin O'Toole 2008

Cover design by DVH Design, Johannesburg, South Africa

Printed in Poland
www.polskabook.pl

For Stephanie, Miguel and Oswaldo and those
who suffered so
and still shed tears,
with affection and shame.

Death, companion throughout my childhood.

Jorge Amado

I
Tributaries

1

"What is your *nombre*?" I asked her. Despite dying to embrace her, I restrained myself, aching, in agony. I saw her appear from behind the hill separating Wilson Library from Minneapolis Avenue. She was walking gracefully, as if she had no links with the rusty weights of this earth, beaming with an honest and clean smile like recently fallen snow. I wanted to have asked her about the footsteps winter had erased, those she left walking before she reached me. And to have time compressed, perhaps in a tear, to give her a glimpse of all the images I had seen, those symbols of my life I wished to flee urgently, tormented, having endured them alone like a pariah, nomad or exile.

You asked my name like no one had ever done before. You called me 'Amor', that's what you called me. From the first time I heard him I felt, *me sentí*, that he was pronouncing the name I'd always carried with me without ever knowing it, that I hadn't discovered, that this is what I was really called and not any other way. No other way.

I can't deny, nor do I want to, that since she appeared over the top of that hill, which hides the Mississippi's flow, lightning flashed in my entrails. A tempest, a wave, a merciless hurricane arose in my chest. I foretold her presence profoundly as if she were emerging from within me, as if her existence had its deepest root in my dreams, as if the feeling of a scorching and devouring fire that was awakened when I perceived her silhouette, her smell, her taste, had been growing since time immemorial. Perhaps I could tell her with overwhelming ardour that I had met her in my most vivid and intense dreams at the edge of a deep and swirling current, in whose waters our naked bodies entwined; her face, lost behind the mist that always appeared in the imprecise terrain between dreaming and wakefulness, that has no frontier or rupture; her voice, that could be heard drifting away as I awoke, echoing for ages in my unsated, ever-hungry desires. Could I tell her that I knew beforehand I would discover three beauty spots, aligned like planets in the Milky Way, just above her Mount of Venus, as if they were showing me the way. My Way towards her depths, towards that unfathomable mystery that you were, that you are, that you will be, with your beauty spots of waning, waxing and full moon?

I wanted to baptise her with my tears or sperm, as I had with Silvia. Tell her, as I had with Silvia, that it didn't matter what all the others call her, what name her father wanted her to take. For me she would always be 'Amor'.

The way you talked about your country, *en que hablabas de tu país*. You told me about the war. Your brother *estaba ahí*; you admired him and wanted to be there with him. Something about it just blew me away.

She looked at me, jealous, longing, wanting to discover the symbols that I had been gathering my whole life without her, sunk in the muddy depths of oblivion, amid the seaweed and conches. Those tricks of the memory that did not name her, but Silvia, the last of the women I had loved.

There was fury and sadness en *tus ojos* when you told me your brother was the only one left in your family.

Later I had a fleeting feeling, something like vertigo. I had the suspicion that you would speak to me in my mother tongue. But no. Your words were in the precise, meticulous English that they speak around the Great Lakes. How much I would have preferred you to speak to me in Spanish, with your cadence and sound. I listened to your reply with bitter sweetness:

Final Silence

"*Casi no le hablo a extraños.* I hardly ever talk to strangers, but you... It's as if I already know you. Where have I seen you before? In my dreams? I don't know why I'm telling you this, perhaps you'll know. I have always dreamt something strange. I am dancing around a fire, *alrededor de una fogata.* I'm *ebria, drogada* or in a trance, *no sé.* Men *y mujeres* surround me, naked, bodies and faces painted. The tallest has a jaguar's face, I'm going to be sacrificed... Neither panic nor fear. I simply feel thousands of kilometres away as if I were watching everything on television. I'm seated on a rock. I look at the stars, a knife with an obsidian blade and a coarsely worked mask. The knife falls upon my chest, blood spatters on my face. I wake up. *Despierto.*"

The sky of the north was reflected in her grey eyes: in them, nostalgia was nurtured by a rain that would fall lightly, rhythmically, to water the fields. The trees' last leaves, brown, red, orange, spotted, were falling, as if a swarm of butterflies was dancing to the beat of a work for cello by Vivaldi. Autumn was passing, that sudden ageing of the earth, and I was just arriving in Minnesota, the midwest state that is the source of the colossal Mississippi river, a place of extensive grasslands and thousands of lakes over whose contours the Chippewa and Sioux joined battle, where the winter lasts eight long months. I had gone there to distance myself from Guatemala with the excuse of studying for a doctorate. An icy wind was biting my hands and face, exposed to its cruelty, but that woman's voice recreated in me the astonishing and agreeable sensation that rays of sunshine produce in the tropics at mid-morning.

"My name is Jennifer," she answered, with a smile: "But my friends call me Jenn. *¿Cómo te llamas tú?*"

I hesitated. I didn't know for certain if the words I was about to pronounce would name me effectively: Ernesto Sandoval.

I spoke to her, dusting off for an instant the creased and yellowing baptism photograph kept in my memory, of the church of the patroness of my city, the carefully extended arms of my mother, the immutable face of my father, the holy water spilt on my head.

"You are not from the States, *verdad?*" she asked crumpling her forehead in a way that bordered on tenderness and consternation.

"You're right, I wasn't born here," I told her with a flagrantly foreign accent. I felt wounded. Could my origins, something over which I had no responsibility, limit our encounter? Perhaps she detected my melancholy. Trying to reassure me, she revealed that although she had been born in Duluth (a city further north, she explained), her parents had emigrated from Scotland.

"This whole country was *fundado por emigrantes* like you, *como mis* parents," she added, moving her hands in such an agitated way that she dropped her books. Both of us laughed, slightly nervously. Her smile softened my coarseness.

"I come from a small place," I told her. I spoke to her about a country I knew, with its thousands of unburied dead and the struggle to change it that my brother had joined.

We began to walk. Without realising, we left the university campus, which I knew sufficiently well not to get lost as long as I did not stray from habitual routes. I had to stop, to express the unease I felt about allowing myself to enter streets about whose name, number and history I knew absolutely nothing.

"We've reached the Seven Corners. From here we can go in any direction: to the theatre, to the library of the U, to Dinky-Town or to Granma's restaurant. Seven corners, seven separate ways."

I thought of Guatemala. The Cinco Calles that can be found at the end of Bolívar Avenue, near Presidenta market. The Bolívar Final where they sell gourds in a basket, rusty spanners for fixing vehicles, screwdrivers, wrenches, patched umbrellas, nearly new shoes with or without soles, where they sharpen knives, sell mangoes in a bag with tangy lemon and *pepitoria* snacks. Veintinuno alley, where you need to walk with one eye on Christ so they don't snatch your cash, a very dangerous place indeed where you could be stabbed or run over by a minibus like those crossing, oblivious to the danger, towards Plaza de la Loba. The Calle de los Árabes, where they sell blouses brought from the workshops of Korea or Chimaltenango, belts of synthetic leather produced in Japan or Parramos, torches manufactured in China or Zacapa, canvas trousers exported from El Salvador, cheap ties, "how many will you take, you know you want to". Botellón street, laid out like a wave that breaks then grows, where you buy Quetzaltenango glassware, tumblers with a bell etched into the glass at the bottom, enamelled pots and pans that will feel the warm fire of the stoves, crockery made from golden and shining china in which grandmother will serve coffee and tidbits to pick you up at four in the afternoon. The street that leads into the Miguel Angel Asturias cultural centre.

I felt nostalgic and uncomfortable confronting such urban symmetry (Seven and Cinco). A friend had warned me: "In any city you go to you'll find a place, a corner, an alley that seems like the city (titty?) of your birth."

But the 'Corners' were not the Streets. The wind – cold, strong, indifferent – that beat my face was to blame for fostering my sense of distance. The sun that seemed to stretch out its shafts of light as far as possible, like the fingers of a hand that does not manage to close, trying to reach the northern hemisphere and warm it without success. The grey of the sky, just distinguishable through the corridor left by the buildings framing its monotonous and icy hue. The careless swagger of the passers-by on the wide, unoccupied pavements free from noise. They were similar, it's true, because of a few things they had in common and because I had seen both.

"Don't worry," she said to me sweetly, taking me by the arm. "*Yo crecí acá. Estás ahora conmigo. You won't get lost. I'll take care of you.*"

2

In the apartment where you lived, you leaned from the window to look at the street. Cars, people, carts, dogs passed by below. The market was in front. From outside came the music of Vicente Fernández, "*at the tip of the maguey, your name, with mine, entwined*", as well as other voices, and silence. The beggars sat the length of the market sidewalk. The world that you leaned over. The traffic, the ladies, the tortillas, the vagabonds. Your face and the rest. The rest and your face. Your solitude. No one in the empty house. Not even your brother, who had gone to school.

You used to spend hours leafing through comic books. They were your brother's and he liked to read them to you; but you preferred to do so alone. You used to shut yourself in your room and turn the pages. The drawings. Imagining what those animals were saying to each other. Laughter. You invented dialogues and recited them out loud. So that no one would see you and ruin your fun. They would grab the book and tell you how it was done (always more boring). You didn't like that. Better just you and the book. Alone.

The first notion of your father: absence. He had been out of the country (what is a country) to study afar. To Europe. Months alone. Grandfather Pedro passed by the house to check everything was okay, that you didn't need anything. Your mother looked at the calendar each morning, crossing out the dates with colours, until she said the "day" had arrived. Your father would come. A commotion. Bath, and clothing that still smelt of sun from being left on the terrace. Hiring a car. The joy of seeing everything moving on a seat that was fixed but yet wouldn't stay still. The airport. Your mother telling you "that's him, there he is, he's not changed" and you unable to understand which one he was. Until he looked up and put his eyes on you and moved his arm, waving at you, saying your name.

With Santiago, you were playing camping. Underneath your brother's bedclothes. The morning light came through the window. It was one of those days that your father was at home and he woke up late. There was silence. You had taken something to eat under the blankets. It was fun feeling the heat of someone else's bedclothes, being in the darkness and finding a biscuit, an apple and eating them and getting out and then putting your head back in and imagining that inside was another space you could also fit into. Santiago put the lamp in, the bulb shining like a sun within those simulated caves. You felt your cheeks tight; you were smiling. You liked feeling that way: happy, illuminated, with your mouth full of biscuit. You touched your belly. You liked it. To feel your roundness and suddenly the little hole of your belly button. Santiago shouted and you were scared. There was a fire. You cried. The bed was burning and you did not like it. The flames. Your brother cried and you too. Your parents did not come. How horrible everything was. After so much happiness, your skin hurt.

When you were a bit bigger they made you walk to school. You knew how to get there. First, the part that you liked least. Reaching the end of the market wall. There were always tramps who smelt bad and came up to you saying things. There were also always bars. Doors with strips of rag hanging and swaying in the breeze. The background music: "I'm just a little piece of trash, let's go dancing, I wasn't born to love, no one was born for me." Bottle tops discarded on the bench and a stench of urine that you tried to pass without breathing in. Then, the church in ruins, the road that went down and at the bottom split in two. An angular house on a corner that marked the fork. You had tied red thread around your left hand. Then you liked to look at your recently polished shoes, the laces like little worms creeping into and out of the holes, your socks just peeping out from your boots, your knees. The yellow satchel you were walking with on your shoulders that carried chocolate milk and french bread spread with beans. You began to skip, balancing your arms skilfully, smiling. Now all you had to do was cross the street and you would be with your little companions and teacher. You would have arrived.

You were at the table eating. Your mother had sliced open

a watermelon, your favourite fruit. You wanted to eat a piece; but first you had to finish your vegetables. It was hard work because you were already full and did not like them much. Your brother finished his plate and was looming over his dessert. He was saying to you: "I've already got mine and you haven't; na na, na na-na" until your dad told him to be quiet. He was; but he continued to look at you. He finished his piece and asked if he could have what was left over.

"It's not left over," he told him, "it's your brother's."

It didn't matter. He reached out and grabbed it. He jumped from his chair and ran off, right inside the house. You went after him, like an ambulance, opening the way with wails. He slammed the corridor door almost in your face. He threw the key outside and announced that he was eating the watermelon. From the other side you could hear the bites and the juice of the fruit flowing. You were kicking the door and insulting him. You were crying and could feel your face red with rage. Your father arrived and told your brother to open the door. So he did. He showed the husk of the watermelon, nothing left. On the ground, pips. You went for him, to punch him. You father separated you. He took you to your room and spanked each of you with his belt a couple of times.

"So that you learn to share."

He also used to say:

"School is a social requirement. But real learning, one does by oneself. You can do it, son. For me, life was harder. I want you to get on, you have opportunities I didn't have. Shush. If I tell you that things are done in such a way, then that's the way you're going to do them. You have to have confidence in yourselves. If one day I say 'get out of the car', you get down from the car and go to the house. If one day I come into the house and say 'I'm here Raúl, I'm here Alejandro', you have to realise something bad is happening and go and hide and not come out even if you hear me shout. Stay hidden. Don't come out. Don't watch telly. Read a book. I'm never going to stop you buying yourselves a book. Neither food nor books are prohibited in this house. Sometimes it's difficult for your mother to understand me. Shut up, can't you see I'm busy. Stop bothering me. When you can see that I am busy, best not interrupt me. One has to run in order to live better. At times it's best not to say things, in this country whoever speaks out is killed. They disappeared so-and-so for talking about such-and-such. Best not get involved in anything. Go to your room, I've had enough of you."

You finished infant school, how sad. No more wooden blocks and plasticine. Also, the possibility of seeing Luz María every day. Intuitively you found her attractive. You did not know what it was about, but you defended her once against Arturo, who didn't know that he should be more delicate with her, more like he was dealing with a puppy. You grappled each other to the ground on the patio in full view of everyone, who quickly encircled you. You gave each other thumps that hurt your fists more than each other's ribs. More than anything, it was just hair pulling and attempts at kicking. Grabbing of wrists, restraining your opponent. He pulled two buttons off your shirt and so did you. It ended up as a draw. You finished infant school and now you would not look at Luz María after every second building block, pausing during the construction of the most important wall after the Great Wall of China that you were raising brick by brick; now you would not follow her with your eyes as she was playing jacks, "two long, three short", and you were kicking a ball with the rest of your mates. Now you wouldn't see her, nor speak to her, ever again. What would you have said to her.

That shadow slipped across the chink in the door. Shut. You had to be inside at half past six at the latest, the curfew during the state of siege. God protects. Shut the door. "Careful about going out after this time," Mummy's voice. Night time, the lock in, terror roaming free. The streets were left empty for the beasts to chew the cud at their pleasure. You were a boy. The noise of the cars grew in the distance and had a particular intensity when they passed by the front of the house. Your mother always pressed her hands to her chest. She said: "God willing they won't come here." You peed yourself sometimes; at others you ran and hid underneath your bed. There, with your tummy on the ground, you felt relief when the vibrations of the vehicle became distant, fading. Saved, for now.

Those faces on the television, of the rebels caught by the army. In a line, one behind another, men and women. Arms by their sides. Looking ahead. And those voices that rose to a different scale, telling their story. They said things you did not understand. They regretted their past actions. Would they be drunkards, you wondered, and did not know. You just managed to see the sadness on their faces, the pain behind the words that simulated happiness, the bitter defeat. You did not like to turn on the telly. Same every time, those faces, those voices, the terror.

3

Dawn has just arrived. It is a cold and grey winter's morning. She feels like staying in bed a while longer. She rises; she has to begin the day early. In her dressing gown and slippers, she goes for the newspaper, to flick through it while she boils water for the coffee.

She is twenty years old. Two years remain before she graduates from university. After that, she doesn't know what will become of her life. She was born in the United States, and since she met Ernesto a couple of years ago that makes her uncomfortable. His dark skin and strange accent caught her attention. He was different from the rest. Out of curiosity, because she felt attracted, she became his girlfriend. From his lips she heard a condemnation for the first time; he accused her government of having robbed his country of its spring time. From his dark eyes, she learned the impotence of tears.

The newspaper has a report from Guatemala, unusual. Page two. A boy's photograph. Distressed, she immerses herself in the gaze staring at her. The report says he was murdered, beaten, strangled, at night in the street. Apart from air, he sniffed glue. The boy's mother, a prostitute, gave him the streets for a home, the freedom to be hungry in place of family hindrances. The boy's eyes, caught forever in the photo, mix bitterly with the coffee she is drinking.

As she reads the newspaper that morning and looks at the boy killed by the police, Jenny thinks the victim could have been Ernesto. Then, she believes she understands why Santiago, her boyfriend's brother, took up arms, turned into an insurgent. She breaks down crying, moved. She would like to be there and to do something.

The child's gaze, printed and fixed, is dampened by distant tears.

II
Back to the riverbed

1

Inside a Boeing 737 a passenger, seat 5D, strains to recognise the chaotic shapes he sees through a miniscule window.

"*Allí está*: the National Palace," he says, tapping the glass with his index finger. He wants his wife and daughter to know. The latter, fair, with skin the colour of coffee and cream, three years old, her face beaming and clothes stained red and sticky with sweets, shouts as loud as she can that she wants to continue flying. The girl's mother repeats to exhaustion that they have nearly arrived, while shaking a cuddly rabbit with a pendulous and rapid movement trying to distract or hypnotise her. The passenger manages to identify one of the lines of concrete that opens up between the houses, buildings, squares, market; it's Sixth avenue.

"Wow," he says, now feeling himself once again in his country. "*Ese mess que tu ves allí abajo* is the biggest market in the country," he says, signalling towards the bus terminal in the Fourth Zone that is stretching out below the plane.

His wife, whom he calls Honey, answers with that nasal English of hers:

"Isn't it wonderful to be back in your country, Ernesto? I'm so excited to be here with you. It must be exciting to go back *donde naciste* after so long being away and I'm really happy María *pueda tener* this experience at her age."

Then, Ernesto thinks of the various possibilities encapsulated by the phrase "this experience" for a little girl so young, spoilt, accustomed to the comfortable days of Minnesota. What type of experience could it be to live (for a period he had not yet managed to determine) in a violent, hostile, savage country. Ernesto is distracted, he looks out of the plane, while examining the dark and nameless territory of his memories. He flies through the multiple images that hit him, lying one upon the other, appearing simultaneously, converging, tearing themselves up. Elderly women with faces dimly lit by the coals of the tin stove. Men with throats cut, their tongues knotted around their necks, like ties. Bodies discarded at the roadside, like bags of rubbish. Masks of Indians shouting revolutionary slogans openly in Calle Real. The carbonised bodies of a bunch of peasants. Santiago saying goodbye the day he was going to the jungle. The smile of Silvia bathing in the river. His father lying in a wooden casket. His weeping mother leaning across the dining room table. The boyish face that he saw in a mirror with an expression of distance and doubt ("What's happening here, Mummy? Why is that man dead, Daddy? Why do I have to throw myself under the bed? Why are they shooting? Why do you tell me not to speak of these things, Mummy?").

"*Estas bien*, honey?" Jenny asks him, sensing his silence, seeing his expression of pain and uncertainty.

"Coming back is not easy."

He felt he was crumbling inside, that his enthusiasm to return to the land in which he had left his umbilical cord, and buried his parents and several friends, was diminishing like a solitary glow-worm in a night without stars. He wanted to think he had made a mistake by choosing to return, but did not let himself. Too late now for regrets. He was back in Guatemala with his family, with all that went with it.

How stupid he had been! Thinking for so long that returning to his country would help him resolve a crisis he could have confronted on the couch of any of his colleagues without having to leave that giant greenhouse called Minnesota. Even bringing the photo, in his shirt pocket, of his son who had died, to show it to Igor or Mario, to whomever he found alive. How pathetic. And to Silvia, if he could even find her, but best not mention her to his wife so as not to provoke a jealous rage.

The plane landed and began to brake. A voice, metallic, distant, resonated in the cabin.

He thought about Silvia; even though he was beside his wife and daughter; he yearned for her as one always does for one's first love. (If only you could tell me in which streets we last saw each other, because I can't remember. If it was the Real, that you used to say had so little that was truthful and so much that was fantasy; smiling ironically as you pointed out that the street was ridiculous because it went from the government building to the Calvario, when there shouldn't be any distance at all between them because they were one and the same. If it was Olvido, that you liked to run along from south to north looking for the jacarandas of the Hippodrome and the brewery's little tower in front of which you had crossed yourself as a child because you thought it was a church, as you once told me between laughs when you were now all grown up and didn't get so confused. If it was Esperanza, that we went along together on the way to my house (do you still remember my room, Silvia, that bed in which for the first time we discovered each other with the clumsiness that was also tenderness?). Or would it have been the Callejón de la Soledad, from which we always fled hoping that the malady of adulthood, the game of old age and the final moment of death would surprise us together. Which roads did you leave me in, stubborn girl? Which clouds did your dreams fly through? Which letters did you use to cleanse yourself anew and conceal the name I knew you by, Silvia: the alpha of the Greeks, the runes of the Vikings, the twisted sticks of the Hebrews or the simple and crude Latin alphabet? Which voices did you employ to call me when you knew I had left: the one you used when you were speaking to me on the telephone and chided me about the distance; that you whispered in my ear when we were making love; that of your weeping; that of your most joyful days; yours, your own voice? Silvia, I was always waiting for you, waiting to gather the courage I needed to return to you, close the distance and revert to you, my point of origin, the bed of my river, waiting for sufficient courage to give you what I could not, to receive what you gave me and I did not know how to keep. Where are you Silvia? How can I find you after so many years?)

"Ladies and gentlemen, welcome to Guatemala..."

Is this for real? he thought as he emerged from his delirium. Am I in Guatemala again? What am I doing back, for God's sake? What was I thinking when it occurred to me to return? What do I do now?

The little girl says she wants to keep flying...

You're right, little Marie, you're right. Me too, but without ever landing again.

"We are *theeere*," the wife says that they have arrived.

Why are you so happy Jenn, when you don't even know what you are getting yourself into? If only you and I could again establish real communication, one that transcends the language barrier separating and uniting us, without finding ourselves half way because we are on my side, as you call it, or on yours, without ever being on common ground, shared territory... What shit.

"*Bienvenido a Guatemala.* Local time: six twenty in the afternoon. For those passengers whose final destination (final destination: death? thought the terrified Ernesto) is Guatemala City, Aviateca thanks you for having chosen our flight. It's been a pleasure to have you on board. We hope to see you again on our routes and wish you a pleasant stay in Guatemala."

"I wanna keep flying..."

This is so exciting! I'll get a chance to practise *mi espanhol*! Arriving at last in this *tierra* so full of colours, of plants, of history, Ernesto, *quéi jermozo*!

Of history? Ernesto asks himself while looking towards the military base inside the airport, and says back to himself: so full of it (not history, he meant), so full of those, he thinks with bitterness.

2

Inside the Aurora military base, the chief of staff of national defence, Brigadier General Jorge Luis Camacho Obregón, in military fatigues, the red beret of the Kaibiles, disembarks from a helicopter whose blades are still whirring. He is returning from a meeting with the commander and officers of the Playa Grande base on the far side of the jungle. He informed them of the president's decision to suspend hostilities against the guerrillas in order to demonstrate the goodwill that exists in support of ending the armed conflict as soon as possible.

"Such a drastic measure is not necessary, Mr President," he warned him, taking advantage of the fact that both had been at a mutual friend's birthday party. "We can show goodwill without gestures that make us vulnerable."

"No," the president, who was his friend, replied. "Understand this, Jorge, I'm not asking your opinion," he said, brusquely, irritated, offended.

"It's just that," General Camacho had said, "for years we've been the backbone of the country. We're winning this war on the field of battle, for God's sake. We defended the state with our lives. With all due respect, Mr President, and out of friendship, I think..."

He left him with his words still hanging.

"You can go, General," without saying Jorge, as he had in the old days.

The Playa Grande base was the most hardened and battle-scarred of the war. It is situated in the Mayan jungle, a region full of shadows and screeches that, at the beginning of the conflict, had been dominated by the guerrillas. Among the soldiers, those who had survived their tour of duty in this zone were feared, respected, almost venerated. The bloodiest stories of war, the hardest battles, the most painful memories, had always come from its environs. Camacho knew how dangerous it was to be posted in this zone; a few hours' long walk from the base, in a gully, he himself had once been near death. One daybreak they surprised a guerrilla patrol that was still asleep. They had attacked the base the previous night. A soldier discovered their campfire, the guerrillas all asleep. Camacho, who was in command of the detail, ordered them to open fire between the half-light and the mist. They took the subversives by surprise. One of them fought back, killed several soldiers. His eyes bloodshot, he seemed like a snake. He even entered the thickest crossfire to retrieve a couple of rifles. This vanity sealed his fate. After turning his back and retreating, he fired, wounding Camacho in the left arm. The guerrilla turned and Camacho, bleeding, enraged, discharged his clip. The burst of fire decapitated his enemy. The head came off the fleeing body and began to tumble, eyes open and mouth babbling...

General Camacho had had to face these veteran soldiers in the name of the minister of national defence, Brigadier General José Trejo Medina. As soon as he had received the presidential order, Trejo called Camacho to his office. He said simply:

"Jorge, why beat about the bush, you know the president's order. Deal with it."

Squaring up, clicking his heels, Camacho replied:

"As you command, minister," because he could not say anything else; he merely gesticulated with a grimace of rejection and discontent.

"And start with 'Hell's Doorway', where you're at home and know better than anybody," the minister added.

Camacho could not say what he was thinking. He remembered that his institution is obedient, unquestioning. What about the officers and troops at the base, subdued by the fire that bites then flees every time they went out on patrol, who knew what it meant to confront the enemy face to face and repel him with machine-guns, he asked himself.

"It's not possible," they said.

"What do we do if the enemy attacks us?" they asked.

"It's over!" Camacho insisted, without revealing his own doubts.

"And what's going to happen to us then?" they wondered, worried, angered, outraged.

How could the general answer them when he did not even know what the hell was going to happen to them, to him, because it all depended on what was agreed at the distant and uncertain negotiating table. How can we negotiate with those we defeated on the battlefield, he asked himself. He remembered that rolling head, eyes open, babbling...

"It's an order from the president, and we obey, we don't question," he said (to himself) brusquely, affirmatively. It was not advisable to say anything else. His military career was at stake, thirty long years (the duration of the conflict) of sacrifices and combat, of nodding and fulfilling orders to the letter, of swallowing his pride before his superiors so he could rise through the ranks and, one day, like that which was now so close, aspire to be national defence minister. Jorge Camacho could be next. And not only the next, but the last military officer to be appointed minister of defence, because it was rumoured (he knew that, in Guatemala, gossip subsequently gained all the attributes of truth) there would be an agreement that a civilian would hold the position. Any old so-and-so, he imagined.

"The war," he thought, walking from the helicopter to his vehicle, the latest model Land Cruiser, "has accompanied me throughout my career." His bodyguard was opening the back door. "It's going to end before I reach retirement." He was taking out a hanger, suspended from the hook between the doors, holding a dark brown suit with a white shirt and tie. "I'm going to retire as a minister." Sitting on the back seat, changing from his fatigues to his suit. "The last minister to be a career officer, the first peacetime minister of defence, Brigadier General Jorge Camacho." Knotting the tie, folding the uniform. "I deserve it, I'm an officer, a soldier, with a discourse of liberalisation and modernity." Combing his hair in front of the wing-mirror of the driver's door. "Moreover, I've taught myself, I've read my quota of books." Dialling a number on his mobile phone. "The president will nominate me, there's no one better qualified to run the army, everyone says so: Jorge not only are you a top officer, you're a true gentleman."

"Hi... Tania?"

Speaking into his mobile phone: "I've just arrived." Getting into the car, the driver pulling off: "Soil and stones rained down on me; but, as you know, nothing stops me from doing my duty." Leaving towards Hincapié avenue, accelerating towards Liberación boulevard followed by a string of other vehicles: "Don't worry, it doesn't bother me." Joining the traffic at the Obelisk: "Yes I already know that Trejo... but he's my superior officer, girl." The driver opening a path by hooting: "I'm coming over, wait for me with open arms."

He switches off the mobile phone. The vehicle is left waiting until the traffic lights change from red to green. He thinks of the distant, violent, revolting jungle.

3

You were calling your mother, but nothing. You were left sitting on the bowl: your pants and underpants pulled down to your ankles; your legs dangling, feeling pins and needles in your muscles. "I've finished. Come and clean me. I've finished. I've done a poo. Please, come." Nothing. Silence. There was no reply. You started to cry. Still nothing. You got down. You walked with your legs together to where the paper was. You pulled off three pieces and did what you had never dared to do.

In her room, knitting, your mother. She was using two needles that appeared to be feeding on the thread. This stretched out to the skein, turning into a ball; God help you if you tried kicking it. Seated at the edge of the bed, moving your arms, listening to the radio. United Broadcasters. Information patrol. Songs of Leo Dan, Camilo Sesto, Juan Gabriel and Napoleón.

Your father seated at the dining room table, bringing the food to his mouth parsimoniously, his eyes fixed on the newspaper, turning the pages every so often. Mornings.

Always mornings. Or night time, very rarely, seated in the yellow armchair. Leaning back. In front of the television. Watching, simply watching.

At daybreak, his shadow could be seen beneath the door. His giant's breathing. Two dry raps. His voice saying: "Five o'clock". You your eyelids felt heavy, but you opened them. With one slap you were throwing off the bedspread covering you. Then, you were putting your feet on the cold flagstones. No point complaining. You felt for the light switch. You turned it on. Then, the clothes you had left ready the night before. Put them on. The shorts, the shirt, the tennis shoes. You went out on to the patio. Santiago always there, ready. "Let's go then," said your father. He was removing the key from the lock of the door to the street as you were coming. Two turns. The lonely, foggy, dark street. Just the light of the streetlamps. The cold piercing your bones. You were all beginning to walk. Slowly. Stretching your muscles. Taking big, forced, unusual steps. Lifting your arms, wanting to touch the sky, your fingers tensed. Swivelling your backs. He said nothing to you. He supposed you would do what he was doing, just by watching him. After two or three blocks of doing the same, reaching Merced if you were heading south or the heights of Cerrito if north; you began to trot. Short steps. Almost tortoise-like, just to get the body moving, he was saying. Exhaling left a cloud of vapour coming from your mouth. With these first steps you felt as if you were emerging from this dream. A tunnel of mist. The silence of the city, big village, that sleeps. One after the other, beggars lying along the edge of the sidewalk, they were never gone. Hair straggly. Clothes crumpled. Missing one shoe. The cold in their bones, warming up little by little as they were moving their bodies. Your father looking mid-distance. Neither scouring above nor looking at his feet. You were looking about ten metres ahead. No more, no less. Nor was he looking at you or Santiago. He was in the middle and it was like some other kind of breathing accompanying you, the sound of his steps less frequent than yours, his trot heavy. The smell of his sweat. "Rhythm, rhythm," he was saying when you had caught up with him. He never told you the way back beforehand, only he knew the route your steps would take, the figure your journey would trace. Roads, avenues, walkways. Going out to run. It was growing light as you were trotting, approaching the house. The daybreak was guiding you. What the dawn would give you was your return. Increasing the rhythm. Increasing the strides. Feeling the blood taking control of your body, pushing towards the skin. Your heart pounding. Your feet swollen. The sprint. The speed. The streets passing by beneath your feet. Your father's breathing becoming agitated. Suddenly, coming into view, emerging from beside you where you could not see him. Making his presence felt, acquiring dimensions. His back. The soles of his shoes. His calves hard, shrinking and expanding. The movement of his shorts as if they were whipped by the wind. His thick black, curly hair. Santiago behind him, small, like a shadow. Growing distant. Both, growing distant.

4

Since Ithaca, no return has been easy. In my case, studying outside the nation, with all its troubles, and being based abroad meant almost completely forgetting about my country of birth. There is something of Lot's wife when one marches off to study abroad: a fear of turning to look back at the place one left behind so as not to be transformed into a pillar of salt. I could go forward because the links uniting me with that place were breaking one by one as my life went by, leaving me now without the fabric that had woven me into the history of my family and country. When I decided to go, my life in Guatemala was practically exhausted. Now I had nothing to do there.

Traditionally speaking, I did not have the customary chains tying me to this violent land. My parents had both died. My father had passed away early in my life, leaving me with an open wound that I learned to live with. My mother had recently crossed that line towards the unknown, as Hamlet called it ("That puzzles the will and makes us rather bear the ills that we have than fly to others that we know not of"). I know that my old lady's death was the detonator forcing me to seek my fortune anywhere that was far away (her grey hair, her impenetrable silence, her intransigence). Going into what was my house in those days (its emptiness converted into an abyss) and finding it absent of that sequence of noises she emitted with an overbearing discipline (the glug glug of the little water jug she rocked from plant to plant, the swish swish of the broom on the floor, the slap slap of the flipflops as she was coming and going along the corridors, her strained breathing) had been turned into a painful ceremony in my memory. I had suffered the absence of my father's figure in the house (his photograph positioned on the dining room table: his happy, playful expression; his surname behind my name like the shadow of a ghost) for long enough to be able to save some grief for my mother. Of my brother, best not say a word. Doing so generates sentiments of rage and frustration in me. Let's just leave it at that.

I liked my work as a lecturer in clinical psychology at the private university where I graduated. It felt like a challenge to this rigid institution's status quo for a twenty year-old to be in front of a group of fellow alumni, teaching them what was considered indispensable for practising the art of guiding behaviour and treating distressed souls. I liked to speak to them about what Freud had failed to investigate, giving them the challenge of continuing to study the human soul rigorously as something like a goal; I invited them to learn the symbols that, according to Jung, inhabit the unnameable place within each of us; to recount the games we all play, or to explore the art of loving or of trying to find the outline between the figure and background (although I did not know of Lacan, I have to admit with shame). But all this was not enough to keep me in my country, because I knew that a greater goal would be to do it abroad, in another language.

I liked Silvia, I did like her; but then, I thought about how she would have awaited my return even if I'd been absent for an eternity. We became emotionally distant after my departure. Writing each other love letters was not the same. Things from the past that revisit the bittersweet innocence that I had lost.

The pain I feel is greater when I remember Santiago questioning me with that naïve, tender fury of his, he whom I had decided to leave behind.

"How can you abandon us right in the middle of the war, when we need you more than ever?" he said to me, innocently, naïvely, passionately.

Even though reason told me they would never win, I sympathised timidly with the comrades; my brother was with them and that was enough for me. Santiago had that desire to change the world, that unpredictable freshness that I had lost after the death of Dad and Mum. So when I found out he had died in a skirmish with the army, I shuddered. He had retained, during his life, a noble, hopeful spirit. He was a sensitive being. He was like a big child, my brother. And he died fighting for a cause I did not believe in.

I had been away for a little more than twelve years. Now I was never bothered by thoughts of returning. I was merely concentrating on my career as a psychologist. After realising how poor my education had been – even though I had been classified as exceptional at the university – I made efforts to bridge the gulf in knowledge that set me apart from the graduates there. It took me six years (more than fifty publications in reviews with an international reputation, several cases with national repercussions treated successfully, and the development of a research centre unique on the American continent) for the academic doors to open wide for me, allowing me to enter a place reserved exclusively for Europeans or Anglo-Saxons.

On the shores of the Mississippi at St. Paul, together with other colleagues, I founded the Centre for the Treatment of

Victims of Torture. It was my contribution to the reality I was fleeing. It was the way in which I atoned for the guilt I was feeling for having left my country in the hands of fools; the shame I felt in the face of a handful of valiant people who had risen up against stupidity. I thought that in this way I could collaborate not only with the compatriots who had emigrated north, suffering terrible after-effects of the war they had left behind, but also with the Argentines, Chileans, Salvadoreans, Nicaraguans, Colombians, Peruvians, Uruguayans, Brazilians, Cubans, Vietnamese, Afghans, Iraqis, Bosnians, Yugoslavs or North Americans who had suffered torture in one of the many wars unleashed on the world in the last few decades.

I always respected the credo of my patients, the flag they defended. What they had in common was that they were inexpert, blameless, trembling human beings who in one way or another had been propelled into the mishaps of battle, unfortunate for being in its midst. They shared a feature that brought them together: their own flesh having suffered the cruelty of their fellow man. They all told of how their victimiser had been a person like any other, had humiliated them with pain, had dehumanised them completely whilst the perverse operation endured. I treated women, men, children, elderly people just the same. Those eyes that looked at me, too, with distrust, pain, desperation, rage and a hint of anguish about having abandoned the life that such misfortune had brought them. "Human debris," one of them called himself. "The refuse of war", another.

My task was to repair this damage, make them as well as possible, try to give them back their smile and confidence in themselves and those around them. I came to understand my patients, but never their victimisers. I was unable to imagine how it was possible for people to do what they described having suffered. I had the conviction that one day I should establish a treatment centre for the torturer, but didn't think I was capable of doing so. Staring evil in the face while seeking to hand it back goodness. It was a task I would not be up for. I had become too saddened and enraged by these faceless beings that stalk my patients' shadows and nightmares.

I could have gone on running the centre. I had been successful. But something was lacking in my life. I thought a son would fill the vacuum. I had one with Jenn, but he died a few days after birth. It hit me hard. More than I could bear. I felt as if I was falling, that I had nowhere left to put so much suffering. I sought help, a place where I could endure this life. I remembered my country, I wanted to remember my infancy. I chose to return to the place I had left, to search once more this land that first nourished the root now cast to the wind.

The announcement that I was leaving the centre caused a commotion. Also my decision to abandon my practice in the United States to return to my homeland, Guatemala ("Where is that? In Mexico?"). The words of Doctor Delsing still resonate: "How can you leave? You have everything here." Could he ever understand the quest that fans the flames of a man who finds himself without a home and far from the place he once called as much. It surprised me that nearly all the staff looked at me almost with disdain when I reminded them, with the pride that is never concealed by a language incorrectly pronounced, of my immigrant condition and pointed out my foolishness (?) for returning to my country in search of my early years. A few (Tim, Brian and Andrea who, as well as being colleagues, are friends) understood the reason for my obstinacy.

I know my wife understands the unselfishness motivating me, although she finds it hard to accept. She lived with this confusion that tore at both of us. Our little Diego left this life in our arms. It was inexplicable. The whole pregnancy had been normal. The child was born without problems. It was as if suddenly he had stopped wanting to live and would just die; he abandoned himself to death. From that moment on, I simply went into crisis. Jenn too; she thinks it was her fault, shutting herself away in a silence that permitted no intrusions. I felt a fundamental need to go back over old ground, search for myself. That death must inspire life in me, I believe. I returned thinking that perhaps the footsteps I had been leaving on the way would show me something about myself. She agreed to come with me to Guatemala, something she had wanted for some time, arguing that she could not know me well without knowing my land, my culture, the sky I grew up under.

I have to remember who I was. That search brought me back to a country no longer the same as the one I had left, which had seemed rather like a big and desolated village. Now that village is nearly a city and the war that marked the country for so many years in so many ways is nearly at an end. We have both changed enormously. The country is different; me, too. Our development has been distinct and distant.

5

(That morning, she was woken by the crowing of a neighbour's cockerel. More asleep than awake, she fumbled on the bedside table for the alarm clock. It was not there. She opened her eyes. The light of daybreak entered through the only window in her room. The garden could be seen through the pane. She tried to locate her slippers with a glance before getting out of the bed, with its immense celestial sheets. Emerging into the world and finding it cold was not for her. The daily struggle developed within: one side, that she called "the snoopies", advocated that she remained tucked up, and the other, "the nerds", demanded that she showered, got ready, arrived early at the office.)

I always find it hard to find the addresses, the numbers, the co-ordinates; I prefer you to give me directions, to tell me where, near what. No use telling me Second Avenue ten hyphen fifty and four; I'll never find the place that way. I need images, not figures.

"You go over Reforma until Tenth street, which exits by

that bank where there are some very strange sculptures," was what Wendy, I think her name was, said to me, with that classic voice of secretaries, friendly and impersonal.

"Those that look as if they're shaking hands, like little paper dolls?" I asked her. Yes, I had passed it thousands of times, but the problem is not whether I remember it or not, but rather positioning myself.

"Yes, the very same. You continue for one block after the statue of Montúfar..."

"A rather old gentleman sitting, looking lazy, in front of the Klee Perfumery?"

"Yes, that way is a little longer but safe. At the first block that you see veering towards the left, turn."

"So I cross Reforma then?"

"Right. You take the street, Thirteenth, that passes in front of the Fiesta. Remember that when you are going in the streets of Zone Ten you have right of way, you don't have to stop. At the second corner you turn left to take the avenue. Get me so far?"

"Well, not that clearly."

I do not have to tell her that I don't understand a word she is saying, that I am even more lost than before.

"You pass in front of the Géminis buildings. Slow down. Now as you get to Tenth street, on the right-hand side you're going to see a house covered in ivy; that's where we are."

"Okay. We'll see each other there."

Meanwhile, I go past the gringo Embassy, just in front of a restaurant with Mexican food. I think I should've told her it would have been better to have brought my mobile phone and once I got near to call her for more directions. But what the heck. Now I am on my way and, moreover, anxious about starting sessions with this doctor who has recently arrived from the States and who, Rebecca says, is brilliant.

(The water, frozen, hit her in the face. Her skin became taut. She let out a groan. She grabbed the soap and, patiently, in a melancholy way, began to run it across her skin with particular care in the bruised areas: the left arm, the shoulder and the right side. Probably a broken rib, like last time. She squeezed the shampoo bottle thinking about her boyfriend, years older than her, who beat her when he was in a bad mood. Then the conditioner, the tears that mingled with the water of the shower. The towel, slippers, dressing gown. The short, rapid steps through the corridor until she reached her room and shut the door, locking it, resuming her weeping...)

Third, foot on the accelerator, radio full volume, Ramazzoti rasping, poor thing, should sing when his cold has gone. Fourth, the disgusting traffic of Reforma, the uselessness of the drivers. Third again and that thing about there not being many mini-vans. Now going through the Sixth oh yeah right, you nutter. Indicator, hooting, excuse me, now they open a way I can take, what are you doing imbecile, your mother, I don't know why they give them cars if they can't drive. Second, brake, stop. Lots of cars and very little space. The mayor should put garlic wreaths on the traffic lights to improve circulation. First, accelerate and I slip in front of the guy ahead. Second, comes slowly, dopey. This time it's not so difficult to find. Third, where is this place. Fourth, indicator, lurch, there we go. The Géminis, the long street full of trees. Why didn't it occur to the secretary to tell me it was on the same block as Pistachos, it would have been so easy. A parking place, brake, emergency lights, reverse, manoeuvre and ready. The little house covered with ivy, not so little, the bell, I push, it rings, "Who is it?", "Who else, it's me". "Come in, don't be shy." "As soon as you open the door," clank, and I go inside.

(She was in front of the dressing table for a while staring at the bottles of perfume. With an absent look, she brought them to her nose to capture their odour fleetingly. She caressed the bottles that maintained their captive essence. She was putting them back in their places, one by one, as she remembered when she had bought them in the shop near work, on Paseo Reforma, the corner with Montúfar: Eternity by Klein to celebrate Valentine's Day. Colors by Benetton for Carnival. Treasure by Lancôme, for a whim. Poison, Hallowe'en. Dune by Dior, to celebrate her twenty-ninth birthday.)

"Wait while I tell Doctor Sandoval you've arrived."

I wait. Please sit down, "No thanks, I'm fine like this". She tells me to go in.
"Go up the steps and you'll see him at the end."
"Many thanks."
"You're welcome."
The wooden steps, the pictures by God knows which artist I neither like nor know, should speak to me about what's happening nowadays, not about other things I neither like nor interest me, I turn right on the landing, a map?, the click, click, click of my heels, the door open at the end and the light that enters filling everything, the trees that can be seen through the window.
"May I."
"Come in, I'm expecting you."
"Nice to meet you, doctor."
"Call me Ernesto, it's more comfortable. Shall we go to the small sitting room?"
"Lead the way, doctor."
For sure I imagined him to be bigger, older, bearded, bespectacled, not like this, so simple, nothing strange about him. That Rebecca exaggerates, she told me that if I found him mysterious not to be frightened, "He's really good, don't worry", what have I got to worry about when he seems even more shy than I am. Did I want something to drink?
"Yes, a glass of plain water that's all, no, no I'm not on a diet, thanks, it's just that I exercise."
"Do you go to the gym?"
"Yes, I like to keep in shape."
"In shape for what?"
He even makes fun, sure I understand they are jokes, no I'm not embarrassed, he didn't offend me, it's to break the ice, I know, I know.
(The only bottle that remained in her hand was Escape by Klein – that she had bought the first time her boyfriend... the first time one of those things happened. She gripped it intensely, looking towards the window, towards the morning light, towards nowhere. She imagined that the bottle she was holding tight was the body of Jorge Luis. She put it

against her chest. She rocked it, sobbing. She said sorry for angering it. She kissed it and told it she loved it... She stretched her arms and unscrewed the lid with a single sudden and violent jerk. She placed the index finger of her right hand on the neck of the decapitated bottle and inverted it. She spread the liquid oozing from the opening on to her neck. She did the same until she had put a drop behind each earlobe, on each wrist, on each bruise. She let the last drop fall as if it were a tear, on her Mount of Venus. She screwed the lid back on the bottle and put it back in its place.)

Yes, obviously, that's the nub of the question. I don't know how he dares ask me so bluntly: what is it that brings me here? If I could tell him, barefaced, there would be no problem, but how come he wants me to say what makes me cry and feel as if I was always tied up, with no future?

"I'm going to the university, where I've been studying for four years, I'm going to marketing classes, they haven't been so bad, I haven't failed, what you might say officially failed, any subject, sure I've dropped a couple, more like a whole bunch, but I've always done it in the first session, because it's not about paying for the pleasure of it. No, my parents don't pay for the U, they live on a sugar plantation we have in Jutiapa. Yes, I was born there, but we came to the capital so we could study with my brothers, we attended a small public primary school and at secondary each of us studied at the college we wanted, I studied secretarial skills for a year but didn't get anywhere, I got into high school and it was hard work to complete it but I managed, it's not that it was difficult, rather that I wasn't interested in what they were teaching me, the classes were boring and that was that. Currently, my job is selling advertising, here's my card, I've already won the sales prize twice out of the six times that I've been with the company, what I do is show willing, it's easy, I sell spaces for advertisements, words that promise the unattainable at a similarly unattainable price, it's going well for me, I've sold to Paiz, Cemaco, Klee, I can't complain. I've also been a model, I've strode the catwalk and smiled without feeling the least wish to do so."

(She chose a long-sleeved green sweater, canvas slacks, green shoes. She dried her hair as she looked at the alarm clock thrown on the ground, its glass broken, concentrated on the second hand that had stopped...it was skipping forward a bit, moving ever further away from last night...it was stopping dead...it was skipping a little bit further... stopping, without saving her from Jorge's blows. She brushed her hair without looking in the mirror.)

"I don't know how to begin because in truth I can't exactly figure out what my problem is. I can't find it, doctor and that's perhaps what hurts me most, it's never been easy for us. For me, the one who practically pushed me forward was my mum, she's a teacher, she taught me to read, to have a clear mind to think with. I remember my dad, for part of my life, with much affection; but later my impression of him went down because he was always drunk when I saw him. What did it matter to me that he drank, at the end of the day everyone does, it's like that Juan Fernando who even ended up dead on the Vista Hermosa footbridge he was so out of it and I had already told him something was going to happen; but the stubborn...What can one do despite being a good friend? But it's also that there's a limit you have to respect, by now in the town everyone was trespassing on the plantation, taking the mangoes without even asking permission, waving sticks as if they were hitting a *piñata*, throwing stones, layabouts, instead of clambering up the trees, it's just not how it should be done – it's really good fun climbing the trees and lovingly picking fruit that, tasty as it is, is grown for export. By now they were not respecting our plot, even the cows were grazing there and they set about catching the fishes that my sister and I had nurtured in the pond. My dad, meanwhile, drinking in the *cantina*, thank you very much, until they even said he's going with another woman, and all the while my mother alone, buckling up, pistol on her hip, so they don't abuse, they respect, the Rojas family plantation."

(As she left the room, the murmur of the water from the garden fountain filled the silence of the corridor. She stopped to look at the three trees on the patio that her mother had planted when each one of her children had reached eighteen years of age.

"I'm going to plant a tree in the house in your honour, whatever you choose, so that when you leave I'll have the flower, the fruit and the shade of that tree so as to have you always near me," her mother had said.

A robust avocado tree that yields beautiful fruit for Janeth, her big sister, who has just given birth to the first grandchild. A slender peach tree that has recently flowered for Oscar, her brother, who will soon be married. An apple tree that simply does not grow despite being constantly watered, in a spot where it gets the ideal quantity of sun and shade. She does not want to believe that this short apple tree had been planted in her honour.)

"You're right doctor, I've been crying, I don't know how you noticed because when one has been a model, sorry Ernesto, one learns how to fake it. Yes, I'm very hurt, but it's hard to begin talking about what has happened, you must know that there are things we would all like to forget and cannot, although we want to. No, there are very few things I've done that I regret, only once, some mischief, when I was in secondary school, I went into the college directorate with a friend to change the records, nothing serious, but they realised and it was, more than anything, an embarrassment to my mum, the poor thing really had believed me when I had told her I'd passed typing with a ninety when for the whole year I had in fact been so dreadful. But there are other things that hurt me that I can't say and don't think I was responsible for, you know?"

(She dried her tears and with her bag on her shoulder went out into the street.)

"They are things that are so intimate, mine, so personal that I tell them to nobody, nobody, not even my sister who has listened to my problems since we both shared a small, damp room in the house in Zone Two where we came to live when we left Jutiapa. She doesn't know, nor could I tell her, much less my mum who loves me so much, I can't even imagine how she would react, at times she's so irrational and her being a retired teacher and all."

(When she arrived at the office, as always, a bouquet of red roses was waiting on her desk. Reluctantly, she made her way towards them. They were fresh, with large petals. She chose one, the most beautiful. She brought it to her nose, she thought its smell was that of blood. Suddenly it became difficult to keep her tears in.)

"Excuse me... it's so hard for me to say this. I know I need help, doctor, but I don't know where to start. What's happening is to do with this piece of paper, read it."

(She shut the office door so that Doralicia, the secretary, would not see her cry. The card was between the thorns. She took it. She recognised her boyfriend's violent penstrokes.

"Forgive me my love, you know how these things are. I beg you to forgive me, it will never happen again, I promise. I love you, Jorge."

Tania crumples the paper – as she had done two weeks, one, three, four, five months before, and as she will in a couple of days. She throws it hatefully into the waste basket. She breaks down crying on her desk, on the sofa, while mumbling between tears and tears that, as always, I forgive you Jorge, Jorge Luis Camacho Obregón...)

"I can't tell you, doctor, I can't tell you. Sorry, I'll be seeing you."

Crying. The slam of a door and the noise that the heels of a woman make as they descend the stairs.

III
Flowing together

1

Doctor Sandoval enters his office, situated in a street of willows and elms in Zona Viva, near the Villa de Guadalupe, a place where at the beginning of the century it was customary to hunt ducks because there was nothing more than a large marsh. In the hallway, behind the mahogany desk smiled Wendy, his secretary. She reminds him that today he has his first appointment at twelve with Mr López Camacho.

"When he comes, tell him to come in, I'm waiting for him."

Wooden steps that sound like the keys of the marimba as you ascend. Above, the landing. To the right, the bathroom door. To the left, the door that conceals his study, a place of scattered papers, several open books, canvas stretchers and canvases, paintbrushes and paintings. In front, the consultation room. A room of silence, wide, a place of reflection. He turns the handle and pushes the door open. He feels a slight breeze coming through the windows as he enters. At the end, his desk, photos of his wife and daughter. On the walls of one side, shelves laden with books. On the other, a comfortable sitting area for the sessions and a painting by Gálvez Suárez, others by Gallardo and Auyón. The brick wall. He reaches his desk, sits. He turns on the sound system. Brahms can be heard.

Moustache recently trimmed. Greying hair, slightly

parted in the middle. English-style jacket. Polished shoes. Gold watch on his wrist. Double wind action, recent model. Martial gait. López heralds his own arrival. The bell rings. He crosses the garden that also serves as a parking area. He enters the house, converted into offices. "Come up, the doctor is expecting you, at the end of the steps, the door in front," says the young lady behind the desk. The heels of his shoes rap on the wood. A man comes out to meet him.

"What is your name?"

I don't know why I ask the same question to start with. I have thought about changing it for one that's more commonplace, less hostile, something like: How are you, how's it going, what have you been up to? To employ any other question, but to achieve the same end, remove the mask with which we are used to covering our true features, our authentic countenance, feelings captured as an expression, frozen on the face. I'd like to dare to say, without inhibitions or anaesthesia: Who are you? In which womb did you gestate? Of which loves have you been born; which hatreds gave birth to you? If you still remember it, what is your first memory? What are your certainties and what are your doubts? From which light do you come; from which colours; what shades delimit you? What do you dream? Which routes are there between your fingers? Which places do you carry on your feet? What things are written in the lines of your hands? Which sounds populate you? Which silences?

But no, there it goes again, downcast, exhaling a soft spirit, with a tone conveying something of defeat, of resignation as it leaves the breach:

"What is your name?" I ask him while extending my hand receptively, offering a precarious bridge across the abyss that separates us. I hope it doesn't seem like a jetty of old and mouldy planks pushed out over waters forgotten to the wind.

No, doctor, you don't seem to understand. You are already drifting from me. I never call myself anything. Perhaps that'll be the knot in this skein. Rather, it is other people who call me things. I could respond to him thus, tell him what I want to tell him, without limiting myself to replying with something that he would not like to hear. Perhaps it would sound coarse to him. Telling him that Jorge Camacho are the words that bind my destiny; but that still I cannot find my true name, that unequivocal symbol with which to identify myself. Yes, I could reveal that my grandfather and father are also registered on the birth certificate as Jorge Camacho. As well as loads of other men with whom I don't share blood and don't know but can find with slight variations by leafing through the telephone book because, as well as Jorge, they are also called Fernando or Felipe or Eustaquio or whatever. And other addresses. And other telephone numbers. I could add that very few people call me that and when they refer to me, they simply say "General, General sir, distinguished General sir", with that servility I abhor but have learned to accept as unavoidable for those who aspire to this position of power. For me, it's a noun lacking content, a silly abstraction that will never be able to invoke the plains full of wheat that I ran through during childhood nor my grandfather's adobe house that collapsed on the family in the earthquake nor the days I sank into the jungles and into the war and covered myself with my own and others' blood. I came to lose myself in the echoes of those questions for which I had no answer and in the fatigue of my own steps, and all the rest of the actions that constitute me, forming me and tearing me apart without pause or pardon. Without clemency or piety. Keeping me awake, depriving me of sleep, of the comfort of the night, exiling me from the territory of oblivion. Of that head that I cut off and that spins in my dreams, its eyes open, staring at me. But that which I did, have done, do, no one has asked about and all assume they are praising my ego by invoking my position, scorning my burden: the weight of images that I have seen and carry inside as a memory that burns and blames, but always binds with those invisible knots to a past that has not yet finished passing. It even foretells the future. Nor do I think it appropriate to tell him with a false smile that my name is Jorge, as Silvia, my wife, does. Then

ask him his name because I detest protocol and do not wish to initiate that absurd series of exchanged commonplaces through customary questions. I prefer to say, while we engage in this strange Saracen custom to show we don't want to brandish the sword by extending our right hand:
"How's it going?"
He responds, if that's what you can call another question that establishes a goal. Instead of opening a dialogue he strikes up, rather, a double monologue. Mirror versus mirror is what you call his defence tactics. He gains the surprise, advances and takes the field of battle. His hand, moreover, reaches out to mine with a certain severity.

His hand is smooth, almost feminine. I notice that it belongs to someone who spends his time leafing through books, writing notes, drinking coffee with bread rolls. I should recognise with a certain battered pride that it seems like mine. I, who consider myself to be so hard. I've let too many years pass without brandishing my weapon in the field, without opening a way through the lianas with the point of a machete, uprooting the vegetation, lying on the mountainside, sniffing the route the enemy has taken. Since that daybreak when I was left injured and decapitated a guerrilla by firing a clip at him. It had such an impact on me that apostolic look, that voice so strange coming from his mouth. In his rolling eyes entering death I saw my own face, my life, a lake, and darkness... Now all I do is wander between papers and signatures, events at which the medals on chests, the neckties, the cashmere, glint and delicate words are dropped with grace with no other aim but to please, to look good. Places where the biggest risk is spilling ink on my uniform, staining it and having to change it.

"Sit down."

I say it courteously because I like to start in a friendly and, to a certain extent, tender, way. I avoid giving the impression that my words are charged with an authoritarian and imperative tone that is inappropriate. I use that later on, when the relationship has already reached obstacles through which navigating becomes unpredictable if one is seeking a safe mooring. Yes, I'm like that when necessary, when I think taking such a stance is unavoidable. I know he's examining me carefully from behind his dark sunglasses. It bothers me that he doesn't remove them; really, it infuriates me, but I won't show it, I will not give him that advantage over me. What he must see is the complete mastery I possess over myself. The mask of the professional that I've fashioned with exhaustive patience. The shine of those golden rings certifying me as a graduate with a masters and doctorate in the study of the human psyche. My friendly, thoughtful movements, prompting those comments that have gained me so much fame. I must continue to be imperturbable.

I don't think he's more than forty years old. He looks young and still fresh. He's elegant, affects good taste. I can see how the profession he's chosen pays well. Me in the clinic of a psychologist! Who would have imagined such a thing a few years ago when I thought there was nothing more than victory, the scene that filled my eyes as I left burning fields, bodies spread-eagled, blood mingling with the soil, the head tumbling, the eyes of the enemy in which I saw my own life. I was still ignoring the fact that behind the bursts of gunfire were the shrieks of the dying. That smell is not erased after the fire, it is impregnated in your clothes, in the networks of painful, guilty memories, and, poor me, accompanies me like a shadow whenever there is light, like a voice whenever I wander in the darkness.

General Jorge Camacho seated in front of a psychologist, maybe you're going mad, they might say, you're losing your ability to reason Jorge, something you've always been in possession of and, when you didn't, merely imposed. What is reason anyway that it's so necessary for one to be anchored to it. Descartes and that path of his that gets lost between the fog and my madness. It wouldn't frighten me so much, if it weren't for the fact that the fog hides things I don't want to appear from behind the dissipated mist. Even so, I'm ready to let the reel run, the grieving and painful reel of this life frequently played out before me like a movie, stitched together, silent, in a cinema with stalls and three balconies, empty, old, with a penetrating odour of dampness, where I'm alone in front of a patchwork screen of white and yellowed sheets. I use that image, now, as a vulgar resource to make myself not feel responsible for having pulled the trigger and stomaching it, as they say, for having clenched my teeth as I was sinking in the mire and shouting at the soldiers: forward, cowardly sons of the biggest whore!

    I wouldn't lay bare this shame if it were not for Tania, for what this young lady means in my life, the dalliance that makes me forget and live. As if I didn't know that I feel like a knock-kneed kid when I'm with her, because what does she know, tender as she is, of the shit that I've been. She has made me recognise that I need help; and that this comes from the person, I have ascertained, who is the very best at it. It had to be Tania because the woman who is my wife now only provokes disgust in me. I don't even know how I ended up marrying her. She was attractive, sensual, but she is no longer. Beforehand I would have just told all this to the barman and that would have been enough. Times have changed. Before, you were just brave in silence, lumbered with your problems, you would bring a cigarette to your mouth and hope that with the smoke you exhaled all the hassles went too, fuck like mad, stick your dick wherever it had to be stuck as long as it was somewhere, and not be thinking about the eyes of people who looked at you reminding you of the death of those you yourself knew were innocent. "What losers", you were saying, "this shit is a war, you're a soldier and you obey orders and from that moment on you don't mess around." After all, you thought you were doing the dirty work for the United States, that wasn't going to allow...But after that, Nicaragua and...it was, rather, the oligarchy. Moreover, as long as confidential sources cover the costs of the sessions, I've got nothing to worry about.

    He thinks he can con me with his attire, without realising that his normal and casual appearance reveals vast quantities of information that would pass unnoticed by anyone else who does not have the solid, inquisitive approach I've gained from years dedicated to unmasking these human games, pulling down false scaffolding, smashing unreliable constructions. Make them traverse the purifying fire, scrutinise themselves, save them from themselves. To have spent more than a thousand and one nights exploring Jung's unconscious, Sigmund's dream world, running between the figure and the background, feeling minute with Adler, being multiple and divisible with Lacan, taking a decision to love with Fromm, seeking a non-existent meaning with Frankl. All that to be able to guide the steps that release him from the darkness he finds himself in, free him from the fears that harass him, from the ghosts that populate his nightmares, the pain that cripples his most noble sentiments, the vices that chain him in misery, the reason that blinds him to the joys of passion. I know it would be so much easier if the client came prepared from the start to reveal himself of his own accord, but how much more boring it would be to take away this pipe I smoke to remind myself that my role is that of Sherlock and the trick is entering the aggrieved's mental labyrinth in order to kill the minotaur that corrupts it, without losing the thread of Ariadne keeping the exit to hand (like a lifeline of my same hand extending out).

Don't you know that the thread is so that the Minotaur can get out after killing you, Ernesto?

What rubbish will I be able to dredge up, with the clear intention of healing my inner wounds, if that's still possible after all my experiences, the invisible wounds on my skin that remain open, without scarring, through which my blood flows unseen, this fucking pain that at times I relieve by saying I'm a soldier and obeyed orders, I saved the fatherland from the hands of communism and all that rubbish I don't believe but relieves me about as much as an aspirin. The men whose throats I cut, the women I let my troops rape, the trances I went into in order to survive, the people that we conned, the traps we set, the shit we lived in for this fucking idea of fatherland. It would be the easiest thing to blame the war, it's what I generally do so as not to feel these goring wounds. That's not the objective here; perhaps it will be and how bad is that, I'll get out of this bloody chair and go to hell a thousand times. I know I'm going wrong, that there's a nagging pain within that does not allow me to feel free. A sense of muddle and frustration that I'm not able to confront and channel. That severed head keeps me awake by visiting me to tell me that nothing I did makes sense, winning served no purpose, that the cramp I feel in my heart is neither important nor worthwhile.

His crew cut makes me think he visits the barber fortnightly, exchanges trivial, senseless phrases, flicking through the fashion magazines disinterestedly while submitting to the ritual society has imposed on its favoured sons. God spares and protects one from becoming a mature, balanced, successful man who goes around with long hair, plaited Sioux style. This has no place in cities of asphalt and smog where one must act according to established rules. Moreover, his closely shaven face, that slight cut near the right earlobe. His brusque, strong, controlled mannerisms. That aroma of cologne, almost pestilent. The way he looked, out of the corner of his eye, behind the door when he entered. These signs are so obvious that I doubt who I have in front of me is one of those Rotarian former colleagues from the Marroquín university that Conny refers to so often – that conglomerate of snobs – or one of Roberto's agroexporter mates, masters with a machete and a mobile on their belts, or one of Héctor's yuppie friends. He's not one of them: that's clear. He's too castrated, too anal. His martial comportment is unequivocal: the recently polished belt buckle glimmers, the jacket bulges discreetly near the left armpit, and that mania of not removing his sunglasses.

"Do you want coffee?"

I resent him asking me something so banal, when I think I had to overcome my fear of even knocking on the door, climbing those clumsy wooden stairs, sitting down in front of him to begin talking about myself, about me, at last. Not whether Guatemala is managing or not to escape from that grey zone in which developed countries place those that don't comply fully with their plans, not of what the New

World Order implies for the army, or the changes for the armed forces under the peace process. No, please, now I want to represent nobody but myself. Can't you see that I've drunk blood, for fuck's sake, I've eaten shit for breakfast, lunch and dinner. That I'm fed up with my wife and my girlfriend can no longer stand me any more because of the violence I carry inside. That I've been shat on in life and now I don't have time to sort things out. I don't want to speak about what I accept or refuse to drink. Sure I want coffee... he doesn't see that, in order to save this filthy bean and the interests that produce it, we beat our brothers to a pulp. More than ridiculous, the question is painful. Shall I make him realise or play his game?

"Do you have creamer?"

"How many sugars?"

It's obvious he wishes to avoid exploring his intimacy, that he's chosen delaying tactics. Prolonging the suffering instead of being honest from the start and saying to me: "Look doctor, let's cut the crap, I came for this and this and this..."

"Don't you have saccharine?"

I hide my rage beneath the courteous and calm smile that it has taken me years to fashion and that I sport like a mask of flesh draped over my facial bones. I press the intercom to speak with my secretary and instruct her slowly, or rather, in a contained way:

"Wendy, the coffee please," while I recline in my comfortable armchair.

Even though Julio recommended him I'll still have to put the ability of this Doctor Sandoval to the test to see if he's as good as they say. I cannot, nor must I, reveal what troubles me so rapidly. It's not advisable personally or professionally. I know they said his practice is absolutely discreet and confidential, but if my discipline has taught me anything it's not to trust anybody. Especially at this moment in my career, when I'm treading a fine line between becoming minister or retirement. So there this doctor has a point in his favour also. They've told me that he's recently returned from studying abroad, which is why I believe that, apart from them saying he's a dedicated academic, he's not very clued up about the unsettled and twisted political situation with all its many intrigues, vengeful insinuations, revelations of supposed destabilisation plans, of the discovery of conspiracies against democratic institutions. The diffusion of gossip that is normal, especially the closer this questionable and doubtful peace process gets to its conclusion.

She opens the door and enters as innocently as ever. Just as I had foreseen, she brings two cups of black coffee, a jug of hot milk, a sugar bowl, sachets of saccharine and creamer, and three silver teaspoons on a tray.

I think I detect a slight look of surprise on the client's face. Obviously, he did not count on my shrewdness, but even in the smallest details I have to make him know I'll always be one step ahead of any of his stratagems, his traps will be ruined before he has even finished setting them, his lies will surface before he has dreamed them up. He must reach the point of internalising what's said about me: no one gets ahead of Doctor Ernesto Sandoval and that's why he's simply the best. It would be false modesty on my part not to accept the epithet. If they say it, I deserve it. In my case there's no trace of hypocritical humility, as in some cases that come to mind, that says 'I don't think I even begin to deserve what you are saying about me, sir, madam, but what can you expect after I've been practising this difficult office for so many years.' I flatly refuse to utter the welter of excuses that are launched like spittle in defence of mediocrity itself.

I can say from the most rigorous and systematic academic trajectory: I couldn't care less about this babble that clouds and drags out our practice. I simply assume that my job is that of working together with the patient and making him go with me to explore the shadows inhabiting his inner regions in order to rid himself of those images that shape yet horrify us, perhaps through his own proximity to the sacred and unnameable. To signal, cruelly, the way out to the light. Call me Virgil, because I take them to hell, bring them back and give them a new land in which to carry on with their lives. I fear, however, that the day will come when I lose myself there and remain wandering aimlessly forever in the shadows.

I'm amazed at the degree of detail he employs even in making coffee. Of course, for God's sake, he has presented me with a range of variables. I have to recognise that with what he charges for his work he has the luxury to do so. His secretary even asked me before serving if I would prefer a cappuccino, an Americano or a Kahlua. In a way, such multi-dimensional detail both pleases yet repels me.

I've dedicated my entire life to this profession. I like what I do. I'm the best and, moreover, I have the reputation to go with it. I have a responsibility that many do not take into consideration, assuming that driving the latest BMW, going on the trips I want, guarantee happiness. But it's not that easy! The real pleasure in my life comes from my profession as a shaman of the global village, being able to confront the most difficult cases, regardless of country, social class, historical moment and age. Not only doing battle with them, but leaving each encounter without a scratch and with victory in hand. To have the gift of entering an individual's existential chaos and re-establishing inner harmony after having gained a certificate in an establishment made of mere bricks and mortar. Ah! This race requires travelling other routes and navigating an infinity of seas, surviving all mishaps and tempests, looking for the way back to one's roots, the primal stream from which all others flow.

Perhaps, yes, one could talk comfortably here. Maybe I could give expression to whatever chains me. I know, frighteningly, that I must be honest if I intend to make myself better. I know it's normal for me to conceal myself. "What is the motive for confronting myself?", I asked myself. It was a question I had chosen to avoid, until Tania asked me to undress, between the moans I emit when we copulate, between the short sighs, between the words whispered in ears, between the primitive rhythm recreated by our bodies – to undress. I replied without thinking about it that not only was I naked but that I was even penetrating her. And she stopped, opened her eyes, held my chin and made me look at her. She said to me: "No, silly, undress for me, give yourself over to me, let me be with the man you truly are when our bodies burn up, when I stop being Tania and become who I've always been for merely an instant because, just before reaching orgasm, I stop being me and I turn, it turns us, momentarily, into Us."

This is precisely what we're dealing with: putting at the client's disposition this accumulated knowledge and experience so he knows, without appreciating the subject's gravity, what is complicated about his particular problem, that he has come to the right place and the right person.

"Sir, as this is the first time you are visiting me, I'll make my introduction relevant. I assume you have obtained references about my work. It's sufficient to remember that I am *the* Doctor Sandoval. My letters of professional introduction are the titles I've gained: the degree, in the local university; the masters and the doctorate in North America. Each session lasts fifty two minutes precisely, once a week in the first stage of the treatment. The full treatment never lasts more than a year. I charge by process not by session, with the exception of the first for which you must pay me in cash. Fifty per cent of the agreed amount is paid in advance, deposited in the account of a bank that I will specify, and the rest when seventy five per cent of the hours of work foreseen have been undertaken. I suspect you've learned that my work is totally confidential and most definitely effective. I'm the best and I work arduously to continue being so," I pause so that he can answer me in his own way.

I know, because I've seen the form he filled in for the appointment, that he has decided to use a false name; it's clear because the name he wrote by the question about who referred him belongs to someone I don't know: Alfredo De León.

"Call me López…"

Why can't I simply tell him Jorge Camacho? If, after all, that's the name that at my parents' request a priest pronounced while pouring holy water on my head. It does not belong to me, it's my father's, my grandfather's; but it's not mine. What do I do to find my real name, which I know is impossible to find because it seeks to synthesise who I am in one single and forsaken word? I prefer to say what I've done in an effort to trace a few lines of the sketch of that inconclusive face I'll take to my grave and that, possibly, deforms the memory of those who remember me. General who wanted to be a poet. What shit. Frustrated poet but glorious soldier. How do I articulate that ambiguity?

"As you wish, Mr López," I say, a little ironically, knowing it's not his real surname, that he has chosen to use a new mask. But, I know I've cornered him. He has taken his first move. From this point on he will have to extricate himself from that mixed condition that juxtaposes revealing against concealing, surrender against resignation, throwing open doors and demolishing walls against being confined in darkness, remaining immobile and silenced. Sure, he'll be able hide under new rags, but he'll go on leaving all those he discards on the way, those I make him shed, like a trail. I will be implacable with what remains of his false identity, because no one adopts a disguise for the fun of it. Every mask we cover our faces with is also, at a given moment, our true face because it hides it yet, at the same time, reveals it metaphorically. What else can our face be but the superimposed and simultaneous totality of all the faces we have used during our lifetimes?

I notice he is annoyed – but I can't avoid it. I think López is the best appellation to use for referring to myself. "Lope" was what the natives called those accompanying Cortés and simply signifies "mister". But now that I've disturbed him, given that he is not asking me directly about my pain, I have no choice but to put him to the test, measure if he's capable of helping me find out if I can still fly with these old wings battered by hurricanes. I decide to speak to him like any other person:

"Look, listen doctor... I don't really know what I'm doing here because all this stuff about madmen does not apply to me, okay."

I detest the way nobody ever has the indispensable

sincerity to admit they need to come and see me, to see members of my profession. I let him know:

"Sir, you know where the door is. If you wish to leave, use it."

"No, it's just that what's happening is that...there's a woman, doctor, who has become a problem for me for which I have no solution. It's a problem..."

Despite the fact that time runs into my account (literally), it annoys me wasting it on winding paths that take me nowhere, listening to incoherent words that never solve any problems.

"If she's the one with the problem, I prefer to spend my time treating her," I say, offended, because using resources as vulgar as that of 'I'm not the problem, it's so-and-so', and if only the aforesaid would come along she'd say it's him, that so-and-so, even though we already know that he, that so-and-so, was blaming her and vice versa, treats my capacity to resolve the crisis troubling him with contempt.

He says he would prefer to treat her without knowing what he's asking. Tania, that enigma named in such a frugal manner, has found a way to live outside the sequential chains of Western logic. Her life appears more like that of gardenias, dolphins, water, than ours. No, Sandoval does not know what he's asking and, moreover, I can't give him what he is asking. I'll say something ordinary, so as not to offend him:

"It's just that you don't understand, man. If this thing was that easy, I'd be singing quite a different tune."

How dare he tell me I don't understand, eh? What I find hard to understand is this: they come here just so that I can then help them play hard to get. Moreover, precisely that which makes me competent is assuming nothing that comes before me is easy but everything, absolutely everything, is extremely complicated, full of entanglements, interwoven with endless further questions.

"Sure I understand, Mr López. It seems that the one here who doesn't understand is you. Time is valuable for both of us. Personally, if there's something that annoys me it is wasting it on useless questions. So you decide. Remember, please, that I'm here to help you. That I must give it my best shot; but that this is worthless if you don't collaborate with me. If you've come, it is to get help. Let me help you."

It's true; he could well have been dedicating himself already in the time that has elapsed to matters I myself have neglected somewhat. So I decide to be a little more honest and direct:

"Yes, you're right. Look, I'm going to tell you the truth..."

Then I recline in the armchair and put both arms on the armrests in order to look calm and receptive, so he thinks I'm going to digest what he is about to tell me as true and faithful testimony. I look at the clock on the wall. The hands show that it is nineteen minutes to the hour; eleven remain for Mister López.

2

You did not like to put on the telly. The same every time. A mustachioed man shouting things at you, the Dictator. He was speaking of God and violence. Of the hard hand that punishes. He was looking at you with those eyes that strayed. He was telling you off. He was threatening you, don't do this and that but this. You were not listening to him for more than a few seconds. The time it took to realise it was him and then turn off the television. You used to go to bed hearing his words, seeing his knitted brow, maddened face.

Your father's comments when he was returning from giving classes at the U: "It's impossible. To know where all this is leading. The students arrive with pistols. Now I don't know who to trust. They say that..." then turning towards the open door of your room, you looking at him from the darkness: "I hope our baby boy is already asleep."

You dreaded it but also liked it. Going to the dentist. It

gave you the creeps, and the rest. Beforehand, now seated in that chair, but still without that light, he asked you about things you liked. Moreover, he looked at you with his big warm eyes when you replied. If there was time, he told you a story or jokes. You laughed. You liked him. Víctor Javier. He said: "Now I'm going to work" and the buzzing began. It didn't matter. He had told you beforehand that it's for your own good, so as to avoid monsters being born in your mouth that would hurt your teeth and make you cry and "you don't want to go around crying, do you?" No, and you opened your mouth. Tuesdays at four. Now you were used to it. One day, you were missing three fillings, you were ready, your mother says to you no, today you are not going. You missed it. You ask her. She does not reply. You sense something is wrong. You insist. She says it's better that your father tells you. You wait anxiously. That night your mother let's you stay up late to wait. He arrives. Dinner. Then you go to your room, they sit you on the bed. Your father strokes your head and tells you: "Now you're not going to be able to go to Víctor Javier." You get angry. You still don't know why. Your father says to you:

"He's dead. They killed him for getting involved in nonsense."

You burst into tears. You clutch your father. You feel his arms hugging you. The heat of his body. You're filled with sadness and the yearning to ask what is all this about 'nonsense'.

A strong, faltering, guttural crying awakens you. You get up and head for the sound. You leave your room. You go down the corridor. You lean on the door, at the edge of the penumbra. Your father is sitting on the bed, his face hidden in his hands. Crying, inconsolable. You want to embrace him and take a few steps. Your mother comes to meet you. She picks you up and carries you in her arms. "Hush hush hush, it's too late to be awake" and takes you back to your room. "What happened to my dad?" you ask, you have doubts, you want to know. And she tells you (why was she so honest):

"Today they found another of his friends dead."

You lie down, rest your head on the pillow, she covers you with the bedspread. She turns off the light, shuts the door, her steps drift away. You are left with the image of your father crying at the edge of the bed. You simply cannot understand.

3

"You'll have to do this while you keep moving", the cold of the small hours waking my very bones from the sleep that had sought refuge under my skin, "because that's how good, noble warriors do it", that night that had just finished covering the earth with its dark caress, "the men who are chosen to propagate goodness in the eyes of His Lord our God", I hear my steps pounding on those lanes empty of all but shadows. "This is how the sun reaches across the forest of the East." What am I looking for when I go on these jogs? "The archer begins the song." What do my runner's steps chase during those minutes before dawn? "Noble fighters give their all." What am I trying to recreate inside with the panting that turns to mist when it comes out of my mouth? "Hunter, you seek your prey in the mountains." The loneliness of the long-distance runner who confronts himself for the duration of the march? "Once." What our inner silence blossoms into? "Twice." Maintaining myself in a good condition? "Let's go hunting at the edge of the grove." The sense that I go forward treading like a deer to a point where the sun's first rays start exposing me, stripping me of my shadows, until I am left covered by the lights that inhabit me? "Let's go hunting at the edge of the grove."

Day breaks. I must go home. Shower. Rid myself of this smell of sweat that I give off like any good sportsman. Help Jenn prepare breakfast ("What do you want, honey: french toast or fried eggs?"). We will both have to leave behind this jumble that, like it or not, urban beings have to live in. She will have to submerge herself completely in the traffic to drop the little girl at school and then transport herself from there to work, which is not really far; but at that time, with that mass of cars, is a trip that can be likened to Jesus with the cross on his back reaching Mount Calvary. I will have to go out into the world again, to the city, in order to go up to the office. Attend my appointments and, of course, begin, cautiously, to map out the strategy I will follow in the López case.

I'll go on testing him. I'll give him the benefit of the doubt. I'll try to submerge myself in his confused unconscious in order to eliminate his traumas. I know my work is about curing the individual, but I must also help to make this sick society in which we live better. I will do my best to cure him. I'll apply my most intensive therapy. I will not treat him exclusively in the office. The treatment will be more active. I'll take him across the water pipeline to the end of the Las Vacas gulley, and we'll talk there. We'll also climb the Agua volcano to have sufficient time and a physical test to measure his willpower against. Later, I'll take him floating in Lake Atitlán to see how long he lasts, for him to talk to me about his worst fears amidst this strange body of water that seems like a piece of sky fallen to earth. I'll be aggressive with the treatment. I will cure him. I'll exercise all my professional abilities. That is my professional goal: to cure him. Because, personally...

4

"I don't know what's happening to me doctor. At times, when I feel awful, I think it'd be better not to be able to sleep or something like that, so this problem will not harass me. But, nothing, can't you see?"

López is passing his hands through his hair. Then, so as

to take the glass, brings his right arm near the table in front of his chair. He drinks.

(It is raining. The pavement is wet and slippery. It's night time. The traffic lights at the junction of Once and Martí flash on and off but don't allow anyone to pass.

No hooting, no rush.

A solitary car, blue, darkened windows, latest model, opens a way through the nocturnal silence towards the east looking for Belice street.

Inside, on the back seat, a man tells the driver: "Hurry, I'm late. The general is waiting for me.")

"I want to remind you, Mr López, that we are here not to duck the problem you're complaining of, but to learn to confront it successfully until it's beaten."

He seems not to hear me. He places the glass on the table again and continues his account.

"As I was saying:

(They go past the church without making the sign of the cross.)

Just putting my head on the pillow, I fall asleep without further ado. I have no problems.

(The Cuchilla, the bars, a whore who shortens a skirt that's already short.)

Whatever happens during the day, I sleep like a rock. Not even the damned earthquake was able to wake me. I just chewed my bedspread, gave a half turn and continued as before until the next day.

(A night like any other. Today the difference is not the point of departure, the presidential house, but the destination: the Zabala base.)

Anyway, if something was going to happen to me, it would happen whether I get up or not. Or, you don't think so? Right?"

"It's your decision to focus on the subject as best suits you. That's what I think."

The patient turns on his left shoulder. He perches at the edge of the chair, uneasy. Is my response, the situation, annoying him? I'm quite tired already, we have had several sessions without any success. He just relates his nightmares with a certain morbid pride. I've never had to treat someone who takes such delight in his own pain. I can't stand it any longer. I could tell him to leave but...It's as if what he has told me pleases him. He does not seem to regret any of his actions. It seems like nothing burdens him. That he is happy in his delirium. And he loves violence so much, something I abhor.

"So, look,

(The Belice bridge, the cemetery at the bottom.)

just shutting my eyes I start to see things coming from the darkness, people. Ghosts. People who are black and blue, filthy, with long hair, their nails long, bleeding, shuddering as if electrocuted, their faces submerged in water, their testicles swollen, women without one breast, without eyes, men whose tongues hang from the neck, with no hands..."

"I hope you understand that the ghosts, as you call them, don't exist as such; they are images we create that originate in our own fears," I add in an impartial, yet firm tone.

López did not even take the hint. That bothers me. He ignores me. He is a narcissist. As if I didn't know that this is the origin of aggression, of violence. What surprises me, disgusts me, infuriates me, enrages me, is that those ghosts he speaks of are completely distinct from those my patients, the victims of torture, were talking about. The ghosts of all of them, I am beginning to realise, were, are, is the face of the person facing me, his breathing, his gestures, his words, his sordid smile, his hateful silence. The ghosts that López talks of, I can see all of them, they are my patients, those I treated, the worthless human objects who had suffered the cruelty of torture. I'm going to confront him. I'm not going to let this pass. I can't allow this to happen. That López continues acting, continues causing harm as he has harmed before. I can't leave him now. I have to do something to put an end to the cycle of torture. I have to...

"Let me, doctor, tell you one of these dreams I have,

(The entrance by the Atlántida, deserted, the Hyper and the crossing at the end.)

... perhaps in this way you can start to understand what I call ghosts,

(They stop at the barrier, the window is lowered and a hard voice overcomes the rain announcing that a senior official is travelling in the vehicle; the boulevard, slowing down, the door opening, him getting out of the car, running towards the residence, using his right arm to keep the rain off.

The door opens, he and the general greet each other with an embrace.)

He breathes deeply, as if trying to find peace.

"Now get this, I'm in like a dungeon, a dark, unclear place lit only by a bulb of about forty watts, if that, hanging on a wire from a ceiling that I can't make out."

At this moment the patient closes his eyes, clenches his fists. I note that his breathing becomes agitated. But there is no sorrow in his voice only pleasure, quiet pleasure. I know that he will describe a torture session to me, I can feel it in my bones. I know he will do so with pleasure. For God's sake, I loathe him. I want to endure this. I want to look upon him with mercy, not contempt. With love, not hate. For the love of God, if I became so accustomed to having to listen to the quiet lament of those who suffered, how can I now bear the complacent account of the man who made them suffer? If only he felt regret. If only he also suffered pain. If only I was stronger...

"At one end of the place there's a green iron door, all stained, closed;

("I didn't think you were going to come today, after what happened.")

...moreover, I can see it has three bolts and a bar. In the dream I don't open it,

("I'm not cracking, General, you know me, whatever happens, I'll go on to the death.")

but I know that if I did, I'd find several steps like a spiral climbing towards a storeroom on the first floor. Damn you, at the other end there's a bare bunk, just rusting wire, and on top of it something big wrapped in a black poncho,

("'Remove him' was what I said to the president, 'for...'")
filthy, half rotten,
("But if you tell him, the president will listen, you're the man he trusts most, he would believe you, General, as sure as I'm here right now, you have a quality many would wish to have, me, as you know, I only want to do my best, for the Institution.")

I'm kind of arriving. I have not opened the door, but there I am, sniffing a stench like urine, faeces and fermented period blood. I want to vomit, chuck up, right there; but I resist. Then I become curious and walk towards the bunk. I don't know why, but I feel the blood rising to my head. I reach out my hand, I don't know if it's the right or left, to unravel in one go the shape hidden by the blanket; but fuck, suddenly I realise it's, like, moving, there below. I stay still, goggle-eyed. I realise that there's a regular rhythm. No doubt, the thing is breathing. I shout to myself 'Don't give in' as if to overcome my fear and see my hand make a fist holding the cover, crumpling it. When I tug the cover, it unravels, crumbles between my fingers. Furious, I undo it. And then, I see her..."

López opens his eyes. I see them rolling, as if they were really observing what he is recounting. The memory was so vivid for him that it would not surprise me if what had happened belonged not to a distant past, but an immediate one. Perhaps he did what he is narrating just this afternoon, a few hours ago. What must I do for this to cease, for him to shut up, so that this man stops? What can I do? Cure him? Only if he wants this too. What is my duty here? How do I guide him towards wellbeing if he's not seeking it? If he revels in harm? What do I do, God, if you exist, enlighten me...

("But if anyone is well connected, it's that bastard, he has contacts everywhere, it's going to be hard to silence him."

"It can be done, General, for the good of the country and the institution."

"His ingenuity surprises me at times, we're not dealing just with him here, but with the network he forms part of, it worries me because such a decision can put the president's position in danger."

"True, but if we're here for anything, General, it's to safeguard the nation's dignity."

"Then silence that bastard, at any cost.")

"It's a woman, see. Scrawny girl, she seems all mucky although her skin is white. Pure cream with beans, I think. She's naked. I see her pubic hair, tussled up; her round tits, nipples hard from the cold. The condemned woman shivers. She covers her face with her hands, her hair is a mess. I push it away to look at her. She resists. Even if I try to be nice. So I punch her in the stomach to weaken her..."

The patient stands up abruptly and hits the air.

"She moans, but gives in. And then I look at her face. 'Fuck,' I say surprised, 'you act like a town's virgin'."

López gives a strange, shaking, sick smile.

I'm at the point of getting up and leaving my own clinic. Now I can't bear it. For God's sake, I can't bear it. I can't do any more. I know what he is telling me. I know to exhaustion. The only thing that is different is that, for the first time, I'm hearing it from the person who committed it, not who suffered it. The phrase he has just repeated puts it beyond doubt. I've already heard it. I heard a woman who was my patient say it. Now I know who caused that pain, who inflicted those scars, who raped her, who tried a thousand times to drown her. He also inflicted pain on me. How upsetting it is to have him here today in front of me, trying to contain my tears, my desperation, my rage. To contain it. It seems almost impossible not to expose myself. Not to break down. To ensure he does not realise how much I hate him, would like to beat him also like he beat her, would like to cure him or kill him but get it over and done with once and for all.

"'For the love of God', she responds, on the verge of crying, 'help me'. I don't know what moves me to say, softening, 'What do you want me to do'. 'Get me out of here, I beg you,' she pleads with me. 'Where are we,' I ask her. 'I don't know,' she replies, 'they took me by force from the convent and put me in a car; when I woke up I was here.'"

Lopéz distorts his face into a taut mess. He breathes out, infuriated. He shouts.

"'Then, you ARE INVOLVED IN ALL KINDS OF CRAP,' I shout at her. 'No, you have no right,' Miss Skinny shouts. 'I'm a nun; for the love of God, let me go.' 'My pure little twiggy,' I respond while removing my belt, and I fuck her: 'Now see what happens for sticking your nose in something you've no business with, subversive shit; now you're going to taste something really good.' And after that I don't even know what I'm doing because Tania wakes me up saying it's her I'm poking."

("We're going to get rid of him, prepare your people, because this is going to get ugly, tell the president, Cadejo, that I take responsibility. That if he objects we're going to do it anyway. Remind him that, after all, it's us who know from within the shadows everything he and his family get up to. Don't even think about complaining. We're going to do this. The abuse is too great."

"That man must be silenced.")

He passes a hand over his face, as if caressing his moustache. He takes a couple of steps. He positions himself behind the sofa and fixes his eyes on me, awaiting my reaction. I must not think of myself. I think of that patient, a year of tormented treatment that made even me break down in silence and leave the Centre so she would not see. Not see my own suffering when I learned that it was still happening in my own country, that had I stayed I could have been her. It was so difficult. And he narrates this with the luxury of detail and even shows satisfaction in it. I must confront him, in my own way. I must cure him or kill him, but he cannot continue like this. It takes me a few seconds to decide...

"This is not a dream," I say, challenging him, feeling the blood gorging my face and an emptiness in my stomach.

"And what the heck does it matter to you if it's a dream or not? Me, all I want is for Tania to stop screwing me, for my wife and her to stop telling me I kick them during the nights I sleep with them."

(He hits the back of the chair violently. He has the order to kill in his mouth and unleashes it.

"Kill him, he should have kept quiet about everything he

had done. Fill his mouth with gravel. Kill him and shut him up.")

"I want to sleep in peace. That's what I want, understand? That's why I came to you, because they say you're the best at curing this crap. They say you're able to rid me of these harrowing nightmares," vociferous, spitting, threatening, with a voice not his own but that of another I have not yet met who frightens me. "Do your work and don't stick your nose in what doesn't concern you."

"This is my work, get it," I say, trying to maintain a calm that is drifting out of reach. "I have to know. If I don't know what's happening to you, I won't be able to help you. Collaborate with me. You have to drop your inhibitions here, overcome your defences, lay bare your mental processes so that, together, we can go forward rebuilding them to defeat the event that makes the rest of the structure shudder and poses the risk you now face that it will collapse," I say, trying to be as professional as I can, less of a human, more of a shit to myself, because I'd like to condemn and sentence him myself, if I could, if justice were in my hands, or cure him, but I doubt that because it doesn't depend on me.

"Let me tell you, I never run risks, none," his features distort and tense up, as if a snake was slithering beneath the skin across his face, "the only one of the two of us here who's in danger is you because you don't know who you're dealing with (You're wrong, I know and only too well. I know your whole history. I didn't know it was you, but now I do) and if you say anything, no matter how small, about what I've mentioned, I'll smash you myself son-of-a-big-bitch (As you did with Santiago and...I know. Believe me, I know you)."

"I assure you everything we deal with here is under professional confidentiality, a confidentiality that I swear to respect. I'm a man of principles and stick to the code I've chosen to honour," I tell him without revealing that, on this occasion, I don't know what code I will stick to: the professional, or my own that will not permit any more of this.

"Look, shitty little doctor, it matters not a fig to me whether you're a man of principles or not; but if you breathe a word, all your principles are over. Understand?"

"Perfectly," I say, standing. "We'll see each other next Thursday at the same time, Mr López."

He reaffirms his verbal threat with his expression. I choose not to lower my eyes. He approaches me, shakes my hand and says:

"Next Thursday then."

Before shutting the door he readjusts the 9mm he is carrying under his arm, arranges his hair. He changes his face and leaves, smiling.

The door slams shut. I hit the chair he has just risen from. I beat it with my fists, kick it, scratch it, spit on it. Soon I am on my knees, face in my hands, crying like a wretch, helpless, like an idiot.

5

That's what your old man was like. You were left in the shadows of daybreak. Amid the pot plants. It was not even five. The full silence of the dawn. The half-light. The heavenly blue sky. The lights of the study were already on. From the patio, through the study window, you looked at your father sitting behind the desk, eyes down, attentive, the pen scratching the paper, constantly visiting the inkwell. Your father writing at daybreak. The dense mist rises. The earth rotates, like a spinning top. You were able to hear the pen dance across the blank sheet, your father's eyes following the rhythm, his hair uncombed, hand tense. The writing.

6

There are cases that awaken something we might call psychotherapeutic morbidity; without any doubt, the López case is one of them. His behaviour, which has not varied substantially since that first skirmish, has been defensive and erratic. I don't know what to do to cure him. I have been exhausting my professional resources with the greatest of effort and have not achieved a reaction. I am at the point of throwing it all overboard. He was even laughing when he crossed the water pipeline at the bottom of the Las Vacas gully; he made no mention of a possible fear of heights, conflicts with orders, anything. He merely limited himself to narrating nightmares in which he crosses minefields, fields in flames, jumps from a plane into enemy territory, takes part in battles in wild terrain, sleeps rough, feeds on dead animals, and things like that. At times I doubt whether I can cure him.

He has shut himself in, erecting walls of silence around his persona. Cloistered in his own disguise, he has turned the defence of his inner self into a habit; his face is a mask. I suspect that, for this man, it is carnival all year round and every relationship he strikes up is converted into a real or potential enmity. He is one of the most risky types to treat because I know he is always on the point of breaking the spider's threads from which he suspends his anger against the world, of ripping the onion skin under which he encloses the hatred he feels for the people around him, such that when his ice melts it becomes not a flowing liquid but a blaze consuming everything in its path (the contained tension, that disciplined repression learned silently, with which each word hits my eardrum).

In spite of the risk his character implies, I agreed to treat him because of the challenge his case posed. López is different. His is another, less honest plot. His scenery is completely distinct from those I have treated before. I would even dare to say completely the opposite. He has witnessed life and death near at hand but, seen from another perspective, both have breathed upon his face and left it frozen more than once. His expressions, although he tries to hide them even by using dark glasses, give this away. His journey through life has been tumultuous and bruising, without much time for rest. His clothing helps him, above all, to hide his wounds, his true pain. But I know I can continue dismantling this backdrop against which he pretends to play a role, with me as his audience, very similar to his own. Or I will fail roundly and will have no other choice but to bury my failure.

Having just arrived at the house, I tried to tell Jenn how agreeable it felt to be dealing with a patient who would offer a challenge, but I think she was too preoccupied with the turkey she was cooking to give me the attention I needed at that moment. I decided to shower and get ready for the 'Thanksgiving' supper she had prepared so as not to miss the celebration that is a tradition in her homeland and for her family, and that she wanted to celebrate despite being so far away from them.

I know she is not completely happy and it is difficult to say whether she feels more angry with me or with herself about what happened. I had promised her we would travel to spend this day in her mother's house in Akley, Minnesota, but she forgot to book the plane tickets in advance and, when she wanted to buy tickets, there were no seats left. When she told me I saw her crying and, to make her feel better, I promised to pay for a private plane from Guatemala to Miami or Houston, which cheered her up for a couple of hours because she didn't manage to find tickets to any nearby international airport anyway, except Seattle, which is much too far. She spent a couple of days in a mood similar to that of her period, only that now it was late and aggravated, until she resolved to cook the turkey and celebrate in our house, which at that time was not exactly the autumnal Minnesota, but it was a house nevertheless and, we three, a family. For this, my wife had invited most of her friends from the American School, where she works.

To be truthful, these celebrations mean little to me. In

Guatemala, a few Americanised people celebrate by dining in Sizzler or the Camino, but it does not go much beyond that. As such, I have decided to remain oblivious to the heresy that could result from the celebration of a dinner of thanksgiving that, in fact, flies in the face of what happened in these parts. Here, there was not even a dinner. I am not going to deny it would be stupendous to have motives for celebrating, with an abundant and tasty meal, the beginning of a harmonious coexistence between the natives of these lands and those who had recently crossed the Atlantic. But the historical facts would prevent me from sustaining a position that, apart from being naïve, would be stupid. It's enough to read the writings of Severo Martínez Peláez, see the murals of Gálvez Suárez or go for a trip in the interior to discover that, since Cortés's troops disembarked in Veracruz, this country has been and remains submerged in a cruel, genocidal war of conquest. The aim of perpetuating a tradition so far removed from historical truth, by making families represent, with jubilation and harmony, something that never actually happened, is a barefaced offence. Because in whose minds other than those of the dominant culture's standard bearers could you lodge this idea that the natives peacefully brought the colonisers the best of their harvest so they could feed themselves, and at the same time accepted the rites of an alien creed.

If this were the truth it would allow only for the commemoration of cynicism on the part of the invaders. Thanksgiving would be oriented to remembering that, in any situation of weakness, it is appropriate to give the impression of helplessness in order to inspire adversaries to offer a hand, food and shelter so that you can then not only defeat them in battle but take their food, burn their homes, rape their women and exterminate them. While they were sharing the table with you they invoked a god that was not yours and, as such, was not real. One more of the many lessons of the Euro-American military academy, as Bruce Miller calls it.

But I know I must leave my analysis aside when dealing

with the needs of the woman who gave birth to my offspring: María Geneva and the little Diego (my boy, deceased!). If she considers it opportune to celebrate this ritual, I have to accept it even though it seems totally ridiculous to me. It's part of the deference I must show towards the woman who so valiantly and unselfishly decided to leave her native land to accompany me in this project I've chosen to embark on, of attempting, somehow, to get a grip on life again (I know I give this undue importance, given that North Americans educate their children to fly the nest early without creating for them the extensive and overgrown roots with which we Hispanics tie our kids to the home).

I also know that if I mention how strange it would be to celebrate one culture's rituals while within another, she would quite comfortably repeat the argument I myself put to her one New Year's Eve we spent together in St Paul. We were together until gone twelve and I went out to light a volley of firecrackers (that Manny had bought for me in Parroquia and had brought in his suitcase as contraband and then sold on at an exorbitant price) on the railings in front of the apartments where we lived. She ended up posting a bail of four hundred dollars at three in the morning to get me out of jail because, displaying how ignorant I was, I had broken state laws by preserving my Guatemalan *"tradishión"*. This will not put me in jail, would be all she would have to say to silence any complaint I made and that I will omit for reasons of ego majeure.

I resolve that the best thing to do is see the positive side of things and take advantage of events of this kind. Better still: I think I can even enjoy myself. At the end of the day, one creates the atmosphere of a party oneself. Sure Ruth, the Canadian married to Eduardo, a Guatemalan who became a journalist, both correspondents of I don't remember if it is *Newsweek* and *Time* or the *New York Times* and CNN and always up on what's happening in the country, will be there; it's always pleasant to talk to them about those ephemeral events that keep the masses awake (moreover,

I'll take the opportunity to tell Eduardo what happened this morning at the office and discuss several things I suspect about López with him). They live in a miniscule apartment somewhere in the centre, in the Pasaje Rubio, dark, gloomy, but near everything.

Johanna is the director of an NGO working with refugee children, an institution headed by a strange, Machiavellian personality called Enrique, who always has an ace up his sleeve. She has an accent that makes one think she learned Spanish listening to songs by Tri or Maldita. I love to hear her speak about the "fousands" of adventures she has with the "twerps" in immigration every time she renews her visa, "that damned piece of paper that allows me to cross that practically ineggsistent frontier".

Jey, who lives in Antigua in front of the ruins of San Jerónimo and is always wandering about, complaining about the national communications system because they are constantly blocking the broadcasting antennae for her portable radio or her cable company or internet.

The shameless Chris who, without any shadow of a doubt, will turn up accompanied by a stunning underage chick impressed by the salary he earns working for the United Nations. This allows him to rent the entire floor of one of the most ostentatious buildings in Zone Fourteen, where he lives as he pleases like a little king.

When they eventually go and Jenn and I are left alone I will put on music by Orff, light the fireplace in the bedroom and...perhaps tell her, briefly of course, about López. In the meantime, the job at hand is that of consummating the ritual of meeting and greeting.

"Great to see you, Eddy. You look well," I say while stretching out my hand, such a Guatemalan custom, to my friend who has just crossed the threshold of the hall door, my house in Pinula.

"Not to mention you, doctor. It would seem that the weather is treating you well."

He pats my back and smiles, pleased. I see Ruth hand a box to Jenn – I guess from the Cake Gallery box that it contains one of the Tres Leches that both of them like so much – while they exchange smiles and cordial words.

"Be quiet. After those winters up north, being in the country of the Eternal Spring would be a relief for anybody," I reply by way of affirming one of the reasons that brought me back to these parts. And I add, to ingratiate myself with Jenn, "Don't you love the climate, honey?"

"Ernesto is so patriotic about the seasons in *Wuatemala* at times that he forgets that *tem bien* they have a climate change in Minnesota that's so pleasant," she says, debating with herself behind a smile and a nostalgic grimace.

"I mean, each place is beautiful in its own way. *Wuatemala* is very pleasant because the weather is always like spring; but where I was born is beautiful also because of the change in the seasons."

"Now you're nearly talking like a pure Guatemalan, Jenny," comments Eduardo, pleased. Ruth complements her:

"Your Spanish is excellent. It's nearly as good as mine and I've already been here two years."

"Well, thank you guys. But the truth is that I barely understand what these people are saying. They speak so fast. I just manage to understand a little here and there at times," Jenn replies, always trying to please everyone.

"Every beginning is like that, Jenn," I pontificate so as not to be marginalised from the conversation.

"But not every ending, bro," Eduardo interrupts sarcastically. "If not, go and ask the comandantes who'll be coming back to this country with all the home comforts."

"Are you talking about the negotiations?" asks Chris, entering the hall from the lounge, his accent nearly absent of the normal inflections of someone who speaks Spanish as a second language.

"Well not exactly; but if you insist..." asserts Eduardo, for whom talking politics is indispensable.

"Look guys, I think the president was definitely very brave to say he was going to be signing the peace accord within such a short period," Chris states in a tone somewhere between affirmation and interrogation.

"But don't you realise, although it was risky at the time, it appears that he's going to manage to do what he said he would," insists Ruth.

"Of course, the guerrillas lost the scant room for manoeuvre they had by kidnapping the Novella woman; because, look, taking on one of the powerful dynasties in Guatemala is a serious business," Eduardo says.

"That family alone runs the country's entire construction industry," I say, entering risky terrain.

"As if kidnappings were the exclusive monopoly of the *guerrisherros*," says Johanna in a firm, challenging voice as she rises from the sofa and walks erect, defiantly, towards us. "Of course the unhappiness felt by the powerful families is another dimension of all this on the eve of the signing of the peace deal, especially with the kidnapping of the grandmothers of the country's most influential families. On the one hand, the construction one, the *guerrisha* kidnaps her. The government trips itself up by trying to free her. It ignores legal formalities. It also resorts to kidnapping (but of a commander, which is valid). It brings down the most prestigious *guerrisha* organisation. They make an exchange: commander for little old lady. The president himself hands her over at the door safe and sound. On the other, the Botrán family, associated with the drinks industry, also suffers a kidnapped grandmother. Nobody knows where she is, or no one says. Whatever can be done is done, which is not much because the lady has fallen into the hands of a gang of kidnappers made up of ex-military. That negotiation fails and ends in a horrendous murder. The operational half of the gang is captured (and the intellectual part? Best not ask). The other half flees. All the government hands over is a corpse. It was powerless against its own mafia. Best stay quiet. As they say here: flies don't enter a closed mouth. Let's leave it like that. This is more for a suicidal writer to publish a novel about. What I mean to say with all this is that the guilty parties in most kidnappings are the same, damned serving members of the *ejershito*."

Suddenly there is a prickly, tense silence. All that can be

heard is the distant rattling of cutlery in the kitchen, Jerry's laughter on the patio, the voices of Conny and Frank chattering in the lounge.

"Whatever happened, Johanna," says Eduardo, "the guerrillas could not have chosen a worse moment to nab the old girl."

"You're right, Eddy," says Chris. "If there's something you might call screwing up of the first order, it's that. A fuck up."

Johanna crosses her arms, covering the beautiful design woven on her *huipil*.

"You also have to recognise that the army knew how to use the information it had at the precise moment in order to dent the image the guerrillas had been gaining," Ruth argues.

"It'll be hard for them to get over this," I say, in order to say something.

"Look, Ernesto," Johanna says to me, "what hurts them most is that now they've bust the bourgeoisie's balls."

"It's not so simple, Johanna," Chris adds. "The delicate part of this affair is that the guerrillas lose the possibility of taking a more strident position at the hour of talks. If their stance had already been systematically weak, now it will be even weaker. Don't look at me like that, Johanna. You and I know there's a lot of unhappiness among the masses about how shallow the accords are. This is more than obvious in the agreement over the Truth Commission. Everyone says so: it was a failure. If that were not the case the Church would not, right now, be preparing a parallel report in which it is going to name the guilty, to name and shame them..."

"There are rumours they're going to pass a law about not prosecuting anyone who committed political crimes during the conflict," asserts Eduardo. "That, for them, is giving in."

"What matters here is not so much the damage the guerrillas have suffered by losing the prerogative," comments Chris, "but what civil society loses the moment it abandons its power to try and sentence those guilty of crimes against humanity committed during the war."

"That is an unpardonable affront. I've worked for nearly

twelve years with war refugees. Those people who saw their relations murdered at the hands of the army are not going to be able to see justice exercised against these wretches, against these beasts, against..."

"Let's have dinner! I've bought some wine I think you'll all love..." interrupts Jenn, slightly embarrassed that her peaceful gathering has turned somewhat passionate.

"Let's go," I say, "you're right, Jenn. When I uncorked the wine I had a chance to taste it and it is...Hmmmm!"

"All that matters is that the peace deal is signed," Eduardo adds ironically.

"Let's celebrate," says Chris. "After all, it is the night of Thanksgiving."

And suddenly it hits me. I feel that I am among those who disembarked from the Mayflower. This is not my tradition. I know my presence fulfills a transcendental function at this Thanksgiving dinner: after all, I am the native needed to make this bitter celebration valid.

IV
Flowing between the stones

1

I agreed to this date, the seventh of December, for López's appointment in my office. A premeditated act: to bring him into my territory. To impose my rules on him. To dominate him in a way I have not yet managed. It could be the definitive or last time. If it is the last, I will have failed and will never see him come through that doorway again. He will wander unleashed through the world like a madman to whom I could offer no relief. I thought the cultural baggage we have both carried inside would today help us rid ourselves of the garbage we have been dragging along with us during this process.

He appeared one minute before seventeen hundred hours. I heard the bell and had no doubt it was him. It had to be him. More punctual than I, because I am always early. Exact, impeccable, the patient who has challenged me most. Wendy announced his arrival through the intercom and I told her to send him through. I noted a tremble in my voice and it enraged me. I was in my own den and I was losing control already. My palms were sweating and I felt my armpits wet. It disgusted me and I did not want to look so as not to discover my shirt wet in such an embarrassing place. It was a coincidence that the clock was on its third chime, announcing the time precisely as López crossed the threshold. The secretary shut the double mahogany door on the fifth and last chime. I felt the echo of this reverberating in my thoracic cavity. It was López's firm footsteps, his sharp look, his martial step, that filled the room with tension after calm had descended when the reverberations had died down. Although I had thought about it and rehearsed it to the point of insomnia, I did not know what to say now that I was facing him.

I know you have not succeeded and that's why you are bringing me back to your territory. You probably think that is always an advantage. You're wrong, Sandoval. You've not read the fine print. He who knows himself wins, not he who knows fear. That's why you've not been able to break me.

At last, I obliged him to take a seat on the sofa and not in one of the chairs facing my desk.

I saw how you hesitated. You didn't know where to signal nor how to deliver the first blow. I'd like to tell you that I put myself at your mercy. I am a good-for-nothing. I want to lower all my defences and reveal myself as vulnerable to you. I have opened all my doors but you keep sounding the trumpets outside. What are you waiting for? That I invite you in. It must be you who decides whether to enter. Stop this game. Confront me and help me. I, too, can't stand it any longer. Go on, I dare you. I've come so you can defeat me.

This time I had planned not to lose control of the meeting. But I have already, yet he, although he noticed it, appeared docile. In this first change of course, I wanted to assert the pattern of control that I had sketched out so starkly in my mind. I know that, perhaps, I exceeded myself slightly, but from the beginning I have wanted to demonstrate that I would not tolerate the least threat against me. I am on the edge: either I begin to cure him or...I have never failed professionally! I am Ernesto Sandoval and I am not even going to consider the possibility of failure! I am, have been, and always will be successful! This is just one more case. I can do it. I must. It is within my grasp.

Do it. I don't fear defeat. That's why I've come. To know what it's like to lose. I want to rid myself of this burden, of this blame eating away at me, of this harm I did to others without realising that also I was doing it to myself. I would like to lose it, forever, as long as I am redeemed.

I have the advantage that he had during the first sessions: it is I who knows about him. I know who he is for intimate, personal, painful reasons that I am not going to mix with my professional life. I'll try to forget what happened. I know all about that, I checked him out, I investigated him. Sure, some colleagues would raise their eyebrows, indignant, protesting that this is not ethical, that we should wait for the patient to give us the information he thinks relevant and appropriate, limit ourselves to listening to him, noting, trying to infer what is not said in order to start winding in the ball of wool, bind our feet and hands and just accept what the patient tells us. I differ sharply from them because I consider that my success as a psychotherapist rests on the complete knowledge I have of the field in which I work. Moreover, I choose to carry out these extra duties, outside the office, that the majority belittle and look upon with disdain, encrusted in that cancerous idea that being professional signifies being puffed up with airs and that those of us who possess the certificate must sit ourselves down comfortably to dictate what the recipe of assertiveness and a rewarding life is. I know my enemy. The battle, then, is partly now my own.

But...and you, do you know yourself, Sandoval? I see it in your eyes: you don't know the answer. I do, although it terrifies you to see inside me: what you are looking for is here.

"Good afternoon, Mr López. I'm delighted to see that you are exactly on time," I say in a friendly way so he finds the greeting pleasant and begins to settle down in a territory propitious for revealing his inner earthquakes.

"Arriving exactly on time is one of the things that characterises me," López responds as he walks towards the sofa. When he reaches it he puts his hands on his knees, pinches his trousers and pulls them slightly as he sits down.

Let's see what comes out now. Look at me. I have lowered my guard. Take advantage of it. I'm here to be discovered.

But I warn you: I didn't come to be judged. I came seeking redemption, pardon, conciliation. I hope you can give me these.

"But it's strange," I say almost innocently, my hands sweating, and I feel a drop sliding down my forehead. "If I recall, when I left Guatemala a few years ago, not many, really, but enough, arriving on time was not what we called Guatemalan..."

I want him to note the difference between him and me. Yes: it is noticeable that he is well read but not like me, recognised by the Academy. I have travelled. I have studied abroad. I was not in this country during the war. I want him to know this. That this gulf has opened up between us. That he feels it growing.

"You're right, doctor," I say, knowing this is what he wants to hear, that I would feel submerged among the masses inhabiting this country. He ignores what fills me with pride: to have stood out from the crowd. Not having an ostentatious surname, having risen by my own effort. I continue, saying what he wants me to say. "Only a few of us are accustomed to such rigour."

I walk towards the armchair beside the sofa. I stare with the aspect of someone dangling a thread, as if the words recently uttered to shatter a silence that had been spread out on purpose, deliberately making reference to what has just been said, were shots. I take a seat with the same gymnastic grimace that the patient displayed. But I cannot maintain his stare. I sense him challenging me, as if he was conducting the session and not I. Who does he think he is? I should have returned his gaze. I avoided it like an imbecile. Do something. Don't lose control. Continue with the question:

"So, then, why are you punctual?" I ask, affecting an inoffensive curiosity, recovering my composure.

I laugh. I know where he's taking me. By intuition. He thinks I was born yesterday. And I've had my fill of this. He's beating about the bush again, as if he were scared of me, as if I were just some poor devil. I'm burdened with a terrible pain. It hurts me, it upsets me. It's as if I had anaesthesia in my whole body. I myself have been my harshest judge. I don't need anyone to blame me. I walk in search of an absolution I cannot find. But what can I do if he does not assume the role I have given him by consulting him. Let him toy around, what does it matter.

"Well..." he tries to articulate a reply, shielding himself, the great cretin, instead of assuming his dishonesty once and for all, realising his lies and his guilt.

Don't con me. I already know very well where you are coming from. As if I was born yesterday.

"Eh...What are you saying?"

I want to tell him, little asshole doctor, he doesn't see that I'd like to tell him once and for all to help me find a way out of this torment, that I myself created my own hell and am burning in it. I can't say what I do normally, what I talk about each time I get drunk, the scenes that are not erased from memory, about knowing I am disgusting. I want to know what to do to get well, to be able to laugh again and reconcile myself with the trash I've been, with what I carry inside that eats me up and makes me feel as if this life is no longer worth living. Could you understand this, one day, you? This pain, this anxiety, this weight pressing on the soul? The shit one feels for having done their job. Maybe you don't know that they trained me to kill, but just that – that, to "them", I don't matter? If it had not been for my mother who taught me the little tenderness I retain, I don't know what would become of me. Maybe he does not see how tired I am from carrying this blame? But I say, in a disgusted tone:

"It's something one carries in the blood, that comes from the family."

That's what I say, although I avoid saying what he'd like to hear: that this is learned in the institution, that they taught me to be ruled by the clock, that I became used to being like that so as never to fail in special operations, when every second counts. If I tell him, the game is over. If I tell him, he would not know what to do. Because I'd also have to tell him that what they really teach you is to get out with your life, survive hell, but they never teach you how to live. Only death, which is the easiest way. Not what comes afterwards, nobody knows about that.

"Yes, undoubtedly," I make notes. "But we require external influences to reinforce what the family teaches. I imagine your own educational background also influenced you in some way. Of course, excuse the oversight on my part, I know you mentioned it during the first meeting but I forgot to note it down: could you tell me again what title you gained at university," I ask him hesitantly, like a fool who takes a chance with a fitting question.

Why do I beat about the bush? Why am I not more forward? Why so timid? I have to be more daring. I must...No, stay calm. Create an atmosphere. Don't risk everything on the first throw of the dice. Maintain a steady pace, Ernesto. You can do it. I've already begun to talk to myself again. Concentrate. Don't distract yourself. I'd like to display the smile that is beneath my lips. López never said it. He, as I can see, who tries fruitlessly to jog his memory, who allows himself to be consumed by the accusatory silence. I know it. I didn't need to ask him to this end. I only want to ascertain if he still persists in draping himself in another's clothing, hiding his face beneath a mask, disguising his raw suffering with translucent rags, or if he has managed to develop the necessary willpower to confront the accumulation of problems harassing him and the guts to overcome them. If he continues playing this game I've set up for him, I'll make my decision. If he goes on, I'll know he doesn't want to be cured and there will only be one option left. Everything will be so easy.

What a nuisance. I'm wondering whether to get up, leave and search out another, more competent, psychologist or to give this one another chance. Why doesn't he confront me once and for all and get to the bottom of things. I could tell him that the title I received accredits me with a licence to kill, but it would leave him frozen. A career in weapons, the most ancient way of legitimising oneself. That which teaches the use of force as argument. Which I'm tired of. In which I'm the best, because I am violent and fearless, precisely because I despise the life I have lived. I would still like to recover joy; but only you know how, doctor.

"Well...let me tell you..." López replies.

Annoyed about continuing this game that bores me, that...I respond.

"As I told you the first time, I have a degree and a masters."

He did not want to relinquish the forfeit so easily. He continues playing to conceal in mist the nub of a dispute tearing and ripping at the real face hiding beneath his skin and muscles. I believe López still does not realise exactly whom he has decided to confront.

"I remember vaguely that you mentioned you'd obtained your degree in political sciences at a local university: but was it in the Marroquín or San Carlos?" I ask, to throw him on the ropes.

He and I both know he graduated in the Landívar with an excellent average grade and a brilliant thesis. He should have been a philosopher not a soldier, this poor devil. He had the qualities to become a recognised thinker yet decided to brandish arms. What a vile profession. But if he puts things right, I'll still give him the benefit of the doubt, I'll think he is seeking forgiveness, to reconcile with life, discharge the guilt he is carrying.

What does it matter if I continue lying. Let him enjoy himself. When you add it all up, I know who I have been and what I've done. I don't want to remind him, I've already had my nose buried too deep in this stinking past. I want to transcend it, step over it. Forget it, and exit clean, new, immaculate.

"In the San Carlos, Doc," López insists, shuddering,

For someone who has not been dedicated to the study of human conduct in every detail, his change of emotion, the slight increase in his breathing, the sharpness of his perspiration, the light tensing of his muscles, would have gone unnoticed.

"Ah! Then surely you know Tacuche? He's given classes there for as long as I can remember," I add, knowing why I have done my homework, that, in effect, there was once a teacher with that nickname, the only problem being that he gave classes in the engineering faculty, never in political science.

"Yes, of course. Who doesn't know Tacuche?" López pretends.

As if this were a question that would bring relief. How sad I feel. Nothing has made the effort I've exerted to come and be cured worthwhile. Everything is lost on trivia. What I want is absolution, to recover my equilibrium and smile. To lose fear, fright, guilt. This feeling that I am a walking shit and don't even deserve the fucking life I've had.

He fell into my trap. He's lost. Now there's no way back.

"Although some people confused him with another teacher they called Chaleco who was giving a different course in another department and who had also been there donkey's years. Obviously, not you," I say, now just playing with him.

"No, how could I? No way," López responds with a false smile that makes the information I decided to immerse myself in, so as to play this tedious game, bob to the surface.

No way, I'm right. Wasting my time, seeing my wish frustrated. If the psychologists who understand human suffering don't work, who exactly is it I must look for? I've already gone to a priest and all he did was get money out of me for rebuilding his church. His forgiveness was loaded. I'm looking for real forgiveness. That is not given to me but that I give myself. So that I manage to forgive myself.

"Well...sorry, but I've taken up some of your session. We're in good time to plan the next meeting. I'd like us to hold two more sessions before the end of the year. My diary is overflowing at the moment. But I don't want to lose the rhythm we've established. The best day for me is in a week's time. We'll have to meet in front of the Santa María de Jesús municipal building. At sixteen hundred hours on the dot. I want to undertake a therapeutic exercise that is extremely interesting and will be beneficial to you. We're going to climb the Agua volcano. We'll camp in the crater. I find it interesting that the journey towards the summit will also be a spiritual exercise. But, we won't finish the session once we reach the top. We'll come back the following day. Moreover, at the same time I'd like to programme our last meeting of the year. It'll be at Lake Atitlán. We'll meet at the moorings of the San Lucas Toliman public beach. The twenty-ninth, also at four in the afternoon on the dot. This'll be about taking a canoe and going on to the lake. Then, jumping from it and floating in the cold water, feeling the algae, seeing the volcanoes, for an hour. Staying afloat. It would interest me to hear you tell me what comes into your mind during this period, as if it were any other session. I warn you it'll be cold and there's something strange in the lake called *xocomil*. It's part of the test. There's no need to worry. Let's get back to the session. How does that seem to you?" I ask courteously.

"Fine, I have some work that day but think I can slip away in the afternoon and be back in the capital again by nightfall," says López.

It seems interesting. They don't say he's good at what he does for nothing. But everything stays on the surface and we never get to the bottom of things. That is what tires me: not touching the bottom. Seeking surrender and not finding it.

With these last words, my real work begins. Sinking myself in the abyss of a viscous silence that would grow until it took over the office, our throats, our insides, so that just thinking about evoking words recreates in the most intimate core of our being a burning, urging, baring feeling that would have all the vitality and angst of one's last breath. Positioning myself in the chair in a way that simulates a receptivity so inoffensive that it hides the violent, predatory character, the hunter's poise crouched within me, awaiting the moment the victim (my prisoner, my client), because of his disproportionate desire to seek satisfaction, comes out into the open where I can, literally, cut him to pieces. I'll scratch off the false skin that you cover your entrails with, López. I'll slash off with one slice the grimace that does not belong to your face. I'll kill the theatricality that you cover the fundamental actions of your life with so that, from the shadows, your resurrected true self, your redeemed reality, bathed in light again, brilliant, surges anew. Or your death.

What are you waiting for, Sandoval, sitting there with the face of a woman giving birth? Don't you realise it's you and not me who's frightened. That you've set this test more for yourself than for me, that I am your patient. We're dealing here with me, Sandoval, not you. That's why I sought you out, so you would take on my case, not so that you could measure yourself against me, as if I were your enemy. I'm tired of you looking at me like that, like an enemy, like the guilty one. I want you to look at me like anyone else, with a common surname, who feels pain and wants relief. Can you do that, Sandoval, instead of your trickery?

I've prepared the ground, set the trap, and all that remains is the stealth and patience of the jaguar, to attain the depth of silence that precedes the clap of thunder, that passivity of the sea just before the storm breaks. I am, I must be in this instant, in this round, the destroyer. Then comes the other task of rebuilding something sturdier, firmer, fuller.

I would have liked to have told you before, Sandoval. For me this isn't a game; it's my life we're dealing with here. The possibility I still have of recovering a little of that lost innocence, youthful freshness. Tania has made me see it. For years I thought that falling in love again would be the balm I was yearning for. Not true. She's been able to see right through me and she has seen me exactly as I am. Aloof. Pained. Scared. Guilty. Feeling increasingly like a more monstrous being, incapable of affection. That's ruined me. Do your work, Sandoval, be a mirror and help me see my face reflected in yours. Help me to be forgiven. Use your techniques. Your words. What you learned. Steer me towards myself. I beg you. Stop playing. You'll get nowhere.

López looks at me, expectantly. He turns to look at the clock, that with its constant tick tock has been converted into an alien, yet shared, heart pumping anxiety as it counts the minutes that strip us of life as they pass.

"And then?" the desperate victim says. I say, because by now I have grown tired of his little game.

I merely raise an eyebrow and put my right hand on my chin to consolidate my expectant look.

He seems like a boy. With this pose. As if we were two youths speaking of girlfriends. It's okay, Sandoval, challenge me but to confront me, not yourself. I know how to do that. I can confront you whenever you like. I've won all my confrontations, that's why I'm still alive. I always thought that my life was worth more than any other and that's why I emerged triumphant. Now, no. Now, no, Sandoval. You must understand that it hurts. To feel it would've been more worthwhile to have died. To be killed before killing. To have the dignity of the loser before the bitterness of the winner. I'd like to tell you this if only you'd encourage yourself to help me. To find myself. To confront this pain that has come to constitute me. Because in some stupid way I still want to cling to life, this miserable life, but at least life, Sandoval, because I haven't got any other, that's why I want to rescue it and be able to find beautiful, happy things, the things it's still worth clinging to life for. Or to let go of it completely, because now I can't stand this burden any more.

"Well, yes... Where were we?" the patient adds, trying to be cordial.

In this spongy silence his timid, nervous words can be likened to the stones that tumble from a dry cliff, with no echo, without receptivity, and break up, disintegrate, until they turn into the original matter they were made from: wind; dispersed sounds; empty space; nothing.

"What do you want me to tell you?" he asks, now more uneasy.

Do you want me to tell you that you're my last hope; that I've come here because I think you're the most skilled practitioner. Now I've told him: the cure was given to me by an interested party. Tania looks at me and discovers how bad I feel and berates me for not doing anything to deserve smiles again. I know that the solution is mine alone: but I also know I need help, I'm not alone in the world. That...Please, enough already. Lend me a hand, can't you see I'm in agony?

My reply is to hurl him to a deeper level of solitude; make him know that, despite him being there, I'm heading for a place where he'll never be able to reach me; flinging him to a point where he cannot possibly find a way out. I concentrate fixedly on his eyes in a bid to penetrate them, cutting his watery gaze with hatred: I get inside them searching for a horizon that I could sink beyond like the sunlight so as to disappear inside his pupils (I am light that has travelled across space) and leave him alone, absolutely alone, amidst himself, with the devastating memory that accuses and harasses him.

"What the hell do you want me to say?" I ask in a way that, rather than seeking to offend, entreats.

I know now that he is experiencing an intrusion in those places he thought nobody would visit because they pertain solely to the tyranny of his darkness. I have just begun to negotiate the tangle of disconnected and diffuse images that populate it along with high-pitched sounds, roaring trumpet blasts, cannon fire. Fetid and erotic odours. A flavour of mango and lemon. A short red skirt. A flower that is opening. A sun setting behind a mountain. The jungle. The city.

Sandoval, please help me. Don't play with me any more. I want to be vanquished. I want to hit rock bottom. For anybody who suffers it, knowing that the privacy of your unconscious has been invaded is something aberrant and macabre. It produces vertigo and desperation. The need to cry and shriek, and the certainty that the life we've lived is totally insignificant. Feeling that the burden on your back, ulcerated from lifting so much unnecessary dead weight, that the chains denying us liberty and condemning us to the miserable drudgery and caustic and painful suffering that make life such shit, are meaningless. They will not yield enduring fruits. They'll perish like everything in the universe.

"What do you want me to say, that life hurts, that I can't stand this burden any longer, that I don't remember what it's like to love?" he implores, tearing at himself.

And to be honest, I don't remember exactly whether he screams it out or whether I merely perceive that this is what he wants to tell me and I hear it flowing from within him, like the song of the cenzontle bird.

"What more do you want me to say?"

Then, I decide that's enough (the sound of the horn of war resounds against the cliffs). Only the hunt proceeds, the prisoner's violent but necessary death (the blade of the sword reflects the light of daybreak; the bloody colour of the sun that clamours for sacrifice so as to keep burning). Quickly, I remove the shield of silence covering me (I run; my feet bend the grass, sink in the mud), to pronounce in shouts, bloody and furious, the following words:

"I want you to tell me why you are lying to me. Who are you, really? Why do you need these masks? What are you protecting yourself from? What do you fear? I want you to tell me the truth."

López bursts into tears like a child who has just been told about the death of his father. I feel neither compassion nor mercy. I must not feel them. Now everything is ready. But, will it be too late? Will he be repenting truthfully? Will he know who I am? Is this one more of his lies? Enough. His lot has been drawn. I say to him in the same tone:

"Get out of here and don't come back until you want to respond to these questions. Did you hear me? GET OUT. Stop crying and leave."

He rises, beside himself. The expression on his face is lean and fierce. Before opening the door he gets a handkerchief out of his back pocket. He cleans his face clumsily. He turns brusquely and shouts:

"You're going to pay for this, son-of-a-big-bitch. You don't even begin to have an idea who you're messing with. You're history, shitty little doctor."

I reply calmy, but firmly:

"You're wrong, López. You're the one who's going to pay for this. I don't know how you think I'm going to be able to do my work if you lie to me. Why did you come to my clinic? And speak up, not so that I can hear you, but so that you can hear yourself. It's clear that you need professional help to solve the chaos you are carrying inside, where words don't reach. I believe I can help in this process to cure you; but I can't if you don't collaborate, General Camacho...Or rather, if it's more convenient, Mr López. Please understand, if I confront you, it's only as part of my work. In the first session I told you that I value my profession highly and like it. What I do, I do as a vocation, and you must know, to your great advantage, that I'm the best. That's why it hurts me that you don't wish to collaborate, if at the end of the day it was you who wanted to deal with this issue."

López, as he wished to call himself, looks at me intensely. With tense but resolute movements, he returns to the sofa. He sits. He reclines. Slowly, he says:

"Where do you want to start, Doctor Sandoval?"

"Wherever you like," I add, sitting.

"There's much cloth to untangle. It's not going to be easy," he warns, sadly, like someone who has been defeated.

"I imagine it'll be difficult," I affirm stoically, and also somewhat sickened.

"No, you can't even imagine it, doctor. With respect I shall tell you..."

Outside, the sky darkens; the night descends and the city fills with smoke. From my office window fire seems to be burning the old Valle de la Ermita. The blaze consumes the year's garbage, just as oblivion turns all our actions to dust.

2

I won't find Jenn when I arrive home. She has gone with our little girl. She has left the city.

"I still can't understand how the *wuatemaltecos* can be proud of a tradition that just contaminates the world we live in," she said when I tried to explain what happens every seventh of December in my country.

"Burning rubbish! This is a custom that should not be encouraged! It's about learning a new way of life that's more agreeable, Ernie. Do you agree with this? I can't believe you do. It's about nature and human beings too. We're doing too much damage to *el planeta*. This activity makes no sense. The worst thing is that you, as a country, approve of this savage act," she said to me while packing the little girl's suitcase, putting in the sweaters that her grandmother had knitted, the cap, the gloves, the long baby-gros that she has to sleep in.

"But...Where are you going?" I asked her.

It seemed to me, because of the clothes she was packing, that she was ready to run off to Minnesota, which at this time of year is covered in snow.

"You think I'm going to my *madre*. It's not like that, *señor*. I'm going on a trip to the plateau, that's all. I can look after myself. Don't worry so much."

I followed her from the child's room to our bedroom (crossing the landing on the second floor and the family room) lugging the suitcase that had just been stuffed with woollen clothing.

"Okay, I'm sorry. It's part of my culture, of those symbols that nourish my memories from infancy, that inhabit what I call childhood, Jenn. Believe me, at times it hurts me that we don't share the same accumulation of events, that we don't coincide in memories fashioned from the same raw materials, that our historical configuration is no more than two divergent currents that only manage to find each other in the delta of a present that overwhelms and drowns us," I say, standing in the bedroom doorway, looking at her as

she comes and goes from the drawers to the bed (where I have put the case that she has opened), from the bed to the dressing table, from the dressing table to somewhere near me, then looking at me with a gaze turning gentle and reflective.
"I like it when you talk like that, Ernesto. Although I don't understand *qué cosa* you're saying. I would like you to repeat it *para ver* if now I understand un *poco más*," she states, crossing her arms, leaning back against the door frame.
"It's unrepeatable. My words, Jenn, like my acts, like yours, are fleeting and transitory: theirs is not our time, although they are linked when we invoke this and then appear in the symbolic world like a sign, a convention, like a revelation that conceals the design of gods who have fallen silent. At this point, I don't remember what I told you; but that feeling still lives in me. I don't know if it would be the same or different. Perhaps, amid the networks of thought, it would be better to keep that thread leading me from the vital context I experience to the signifying language I use taut, so as to stay afloat. Perhaps the best thing is to go back to look for what's been said, between the tides and tempests, not over a few minutes but several epochs, so we can find and discover calmly that which names and transcends us."
I get close to her. I embrace her.
"Go on, please," she says to me.
"Where to? Towards wherever we find? Let's admit it: we have two distinct births, Jenn, and long paths that did not cross the same territory (yours were the lakes and snowdrifts while mine were...how can I tell you without hurting myself?). When we were children, to you the beginning of winter used to signify the challenge of seeing which of your friends were first to cross the frozen lake three blocks from your house, in Como Park. You had to take a risk to cross, knowing it was probable that the ice was not hard enough to support the adventurer's weight. Do you remember that once you challenged me to cross as if we were still kids? That I accepted this infantile challenge, at my twenty-something years of age, and told you I had never walked on

frozen ice before as my legs quivered and crunched on the cracking surface. I remember you at the edge, with that red coat you liked so much; at first laughing, then worried that it would give way and you'd have to drag me out with hypothermia and the help of the fire brigade, if they got me out at all. I tell you this now, my love: I did it to try and go back in time (how absurd!) and experience, just a little, of what it was like to be a boy during winter.

    Jenn separates from my arms. She walks slowly towards the bed. She sits against the headboard, with her legs crossed in the yoga style. I remain in the doorway, a little less warm.

"I'm sorry," she says.
"What for, Jenny?"
"Not having been here..."
"Where?"
"You told me once that when you were a boy you liked to go out to light firecrackers – *cuates*?"
"*Cu-e-tes*, Jenn."
"I still don't understand. Are you referring to this custom?"
"No, the one on Saturday is about something more than going out and lighting firecrackers. It's the rite that opens the way to the Christmas festivities. It's the fire we must invoke collectively to arrive cleansed at the festival. The burning of the rubbish is just what you see. To know its significance we must be ready to immerse ourselves in what can't be seen. But it's the fire, Jenn. Around it, we will tell of the misfortunes of the year that's passing, of the cycle that dies, we'll drink a concoction prepared with fruit and liquor, peel maize wrapped in a leaf and then eat our sacrament that neither pardons nor saves because, I want you to know, girl, we are a people cursed by the gods we abandoned for a false promise of love and a story we found it easy to identify with because they, also, unjustly nailed us to the cross," I say, feeling ever less understood.

"You see? It's what I was telling you," she says, without me being able to understand what she means.

"Look, Jenn," I interrupt, before losing hope, "for us, considerations about preserving the future of the planet have no substance because we don't think of history as a definitive line traced from a monastery so that we throw up our arms awaiting the second coming of a Messiah who will save us from the damage caused by his own followers. Our world, Jenn, was always on the edge of collapse. The earthquakes and the work of generations crumble; it pushes us to migrate and start afresh. We're here because we settled right upon the fire, upon the open mouths of the volcanoes, the place where the earthquake demon Cabracán was buried. We know we are finite, and that amuses us. We know the stars and the gods feed on our blood, need our sacrifice. And ecological criticisms of our cultural events are no more than another aggression by those who continue to lack respect for us. Aren't those who dictate perhaps the very same ones who caused the damage they now think about trying to reverse? I'm fire, Jenn, and as such I will also be smoke. They can condemn me if they wish. I'll continue dancing around the flames and building my life in the folds of the volcanoes."

"But that's precisely what I want to go and see with our daughter, how the people on the plateau live. I believe that, by doing so, I can understand you better and give you space and time for you to work on your things."

"Well, go and see. What you'll see is also me. Because how else can I make you understand, Jenny, about these – two? – bloods doing battle in the dark passages of my insides, with an amazing intensity, a dilated fury and a loathed disequilibrium. This is my blood, my love: a junction of torrents, pregnant with discord."

3

You were coming on a flight from Chicago. You boarded the plane right on midnight. You were exhausted. The emotion was subsiding. The tension of the new scenario. You were returning.

A rumble in your stomach shook you. A force, beast, demon, trapped in your entrails was looking for a way out. It poked into the cavities with slaps, feeding off anxiety and rising by shoving. Burning and tearing, violently, atrociously, it passed through. You felt it sweeping across your throat. It escaped in the form of a shout. You opened your eyes. You woke up. Four-forty on the clock. You feel as if you are suffocating. Suddenly, tears. You do not know why. You try to go back to sleep, without succeeding. Cold. Something has perturbed you. Now there will be no comfort.

You land at the airport. You go into the street. Two, three, five taxi drivers offer you their services. "They're coming for me," you say. Hand on suitcase. The straps of the backpack sink upon your shoulders. Pain. Fatigue. They do not show. It is getting late, it seems strange to you.

Your brother appears at the wheel of your father's car. His expression hard, stoical. Six in the morning. Mother in the back, silent. The vehicle stops. They open the rear door. You get in and sit down. The tyres spin. On your way. Mum keeps looking at you and does not speak. Inside, you feel your heart misses a beat. Ants on your feet. Santiago stops. He turns and looks at you. "Dad has died," he says. You open the door of the car. You want to escape these words that disgust you, that you reject. You drop to the pavement.

The route becomes misty with tears. It was a sunny morning but to you the journey seemed rainy. The civic centre. Cathedral. Streets and gate that opens. You put one foot on the ground while the vehicle is still moving. You run to your father's room. The bed is unmade. You put your hand on the mattress, between the blankets. Warm. The kitchen, he has to be in the kitchen. Nothing. You run towards the study, to look for him among the books. You cross the doorway and look at the shelves. You shout out your father's name and your cry dies in a distant echo. Your legs suddenly become weak. You want to run back to the patio again. But you can bear no more. You fall down, amid the flowers and the bushes. Groans. You clench the earth in your fists and feel rage. Ire. Impotence. "What am I going to do," you ask yourself, and no one replies.

The journey to the morgue. At the end of Twentieth street, beside the General Cemetery. As they say at the moment of death: "Reaching the end of Twentieth street". You drive, but you remember nothing. It was as if you had just arrived, without driving, without having to cross intersections, overtake other vehicles. You get out. You enter the building. You emit a sound similar to the name of your father to a nurse and she points to a door. Before you get there, it opens and a doctor comes out. You ask. The doctor says:

"He's there."

He holds the door for you. You enter. You do not know what you will find. A few steps inside, you realise. The naked body of your father, on a concrete slab. Naked. His eyes are shut as if he were sleeping, but there is a sensation of cold that gets beneath your flesh and surges beneath the skin. Flavour of rust in the mouth. Tongue as if it were asleep. Heavy hands. Feet that advance in a clumsy way towards a body that is no longer that of your father, but at the same time still is. You see stitches across the chest. Without being able to contain yourself, you put a hand on them and trace them along their length. From the last stitch on the right towards above the left nipple. The tears well up in your eyes. Your vision clouds over. You stroke his forehead. You emit strange, straining sounds from your throat. You sigh. You go back to stroking his forehead. He seems to be at peace. You bend down and kiss his lips. The contact with the frozen skin congeals your blood. You rise. You throw your head back and shout. You kiss his lips again and realise that he has died. That your father has died. That he is no longer alive. That he's dead, for fuck's sake. He's dead. He died, and that it hurts you and that now you cannot even tell him you love him despite everything.

You return to the light of day. Organising what is possible. You think of the people who have to be told, what has to be done, but only manage to sit on the edge of the bench in the mortuary car park. Santiago is with you. You hug each other. You take advantage to bury your face in his shoulder and cry without the need for subterfuge. Brothers, grief-stricken.

Santiago was the first to see him dead. They were going along on bicycles together heading for Huehuetenango. They had just left the ring road and entered Roosevelt. Santiago was ahead and Dad behind. Santiago hears a noise, something brushing his head as it flies by; he thinks it is a stone or something. Beside them, a vehicle passes at a scandalous speed. Ten steps away he sees the body of his father lying on the verge. He shouts out terrified. It can't be, he thinks, if Dad was behind me. He turns. The empty highway. The silence and the darkness of daybreak. Santiago dismounts. He approaches his father's corpse. His face disfigured by the blow. His body contorted. He speaks to him as if he were going to reply, but nothing. Blood comes from his mouth, not words. Santiago clutches his head. He kneels and cries, in screeches, with no self-control.

Some marathon runners we knew then pass by. They are surprised to see a youth crying and kneeling in front of another man. An accident, they suppose, and approach. They recognise Santiago and, as they get nearer, moreover, his father. They try to find out what happened. Santiago only manages to sob; he does not answer them, as if they were not even there. They go to a public telephone. They report it.

You choose the clothes your father is going to be buried in. You realise you are not going to be able to do it. You hand it over to Santiago.

The house begins to fill with people your father knew. The family helps to bring chairs, serve coffee, tasks like that. You are in your room, surrounded by friends, quiet, without being able to articulate the mystery, the fear that corrupts you.

You go up to the coffin several times. Paper and pencil in hand. You intend to write something to read at the funeral. Something that summarises what your father was like, that says his life was worthwhile, what he learned in his journey through the world. Every time you do so, you cry. You wet the paper with your tears. You realise how useless it is to write compared with the intensity of your emotions. Words are nothing.

When you arrive at the cemetery you take turns to carry the casket. You put your shoulder beneath the box. You feel the weight of the world. Your feet sink into the sidewalk. You take several steps. Your eyes are clouded, you cannot see. You fall to the ground. You cannot deal with the weight of death.

They place him in the tomb. Psalms are sung while the opening of the niche is bricked over. You remain, sobbing, with your right arm up and fist clenched. You did not know what else to do. Your father has died. You do not know what to do. What. Your father has died. Now he is even buried.

4

I have been reading some things about Guatemala, trying to understand its conflictive history. It has surprised me a great deal to learn how much the United States has been involved and how they have been the cause of much of the problem. I am angry that all this has been hidden from us, continues to be hidden from us.

Accompanying Ernesto to search for his roots helps me rebel a little against what I have been like, all of which implies pain, and ignorance of other ways of life. Now I understand your search a bit better, Ernesto, all that was so hard for you to tell me when you were beginning to speak about who you were. Yes, being here, in this little town on the plateau, amidst these indigenous women who spend their day making tortillas around the fire. Aren't these the towns you were talking about? These are the people for whom you decided to dedicate your life. Now I understand better.

I'm learning to weave, to mix the threads. The clothing, so full of colours and animals, like your country, which you told me was full of both joy and horror. I know why you were telling me this. The clothes help me understand. I see it so clearly in the face of Juana – a sad expression, like extinguished tenderness, her lips only just revealing the smile traced with the passing of the days, in such contrast with the prettiness and vividness of her *guipil*. And not only Juana; also Remigia and Natividad and many women in the hamlet. You're right: it's not only the women who are sad. Why do I think Manlio is on the verge of crying every time he speaks? Why do I feel something akin to tension tearing at Hortensio when I hear him speaking of Evangelio? A vast, accumulated suffering, you once said to me.

I have just read a little of what I wrote and it surprises me to realise that I feel I'm expressing myself myself better in Spanish than in the language of my birthplace. I have read several books in English written by people who didn't grow up speaking the language and their usage is nearly perfect. It's rare to find a book written by someone who has abandoned their English to express themselves in another language. Will it be necessary to speak what I speak in order to make myself heard? Because I don't speak Spanish as well as English, but I can write in them equally well; I can also understand much of what I read.

Today I learned to give form with thread to a little bird on the *guipil* I'm weaving. It requires a lot of work and patience to join the threads, give them a shape in which the drawing appears, despite being interwoven, about to fly away, free, a little warrior. It frustrated me a little just because it took so much work. I can also tell you that I have abandoned my canvas slacks for this typical costume. Whoever said our legs should be trapped in that stupid fabric? I now feel more full of life, like the spring, with those designs that are so pretty. I've managed to speak a few words in the indigenous language; not as many as you, but enough.

    I miss you. I'm always thinking of you. I ask myself if you can feel the energy I am sending you so that you know you're within me. I think about you a great deal. Hopefully, when you come I can tell you all this, Ernesto, my love.

V
Final Silence

I am at the edge of the lake of the Tzutuhiles, Atitlán, likely site of the lost city of Tepepul, in an emaciated and stunted pine forest, where the locals gather to celebrate ancestral ceremonies, among the rocks and shadows, opening their path with the light of the *ocote* trees (that are confused from a distance with incandescent insects). The site smells of *pom* miracle dust and *chilca* healing herbs and is not frequented by tourists. It is sacred ground for those who still communicate in the language of the water and birds. It is here that I wait. On foot, my view fixed on the *xocomil* whirlpools, while López, Camacho, or whatever he wants to call himself, arrives. We have agreed to meet at this spot, from where you can see the local public beach, at four in the afternoon. I have rented a canoe that I will pilot to the middle of the lake for the day's session. We will float in this freezing water. What López fears to confront will surface there. The test will be a rite of passage, like a baptism that cures the patient; metaphorically, so that he drinks from the water of forgetfulness and is born again into life. If it is any other way, I will have failed. But I don't think so, today more than any other day, I feel close to something I don't have a name for. This has been one of my most difficult cases, but I have succeeded. I am on the verge of succeeding. To return to someone the innocence necessary for them to regain their smile. I had moments of doubt, I had never confronted anything like it. But I did it, with patience and tenacity. He has been cleansing himself, recuperating the tenderness tarnished throughout his life by bloodshed.

    I see him, sitting, between the shadows. His eyes are fixed on the blue of the sky that is lost on the horizon and melds with the dark green of the volcanoes surrounding the lake and the turquoise of the water. He was there, as ever. Waiting for me. I have to admit he is a type given over completely to his work. No matter how much I confronted and challenged him, he knew how to show willingness and continue with his head held high. I know it has been hard for him, but he has managed to go forward dragging me along. I feel much better than I have felt in many years. His methods are strange but effective. They hit the spot in a precise and painful way, but one that alleviates. I've managed to find myself a couple of times. I've cried like a child, with innocence, with pain, with purity, even with a runny nose. I've broken down on seeing myself amid the fog of my memories. I've touched wounds I thought had closed up. I have visited my own hell. I've been surrounded by a chorus of laments, naked weeping, sharp screeches. Faces I thought I had buried, mutilated bodies, children ripped from the wombs of their mothers to be abandoned unto death, have appeared before me. And I have asked them for forgiveness. With tears, breaking down, on my knees, writhing on the floor with pain, pulling out my hair, beating my chest, I have asked for forgiveness. I have seen those harshly staring faces become indulgent with me, little by little, forgiving my stupidity, ignorance and violence. But it is not all over. I know there is still a little left for me to do in order to exit. That I need to feel new water running across my forehead and cleansing me, someone saying a word that absolves and transforms me. That there is a little left to do for me to gain the forgiveness that costs so much, the forgiveness you grant yourself so as to reconcile yourself to what you have been. I hope that by floating in the middle of the lake I'll manage to achieve what I have not been able to on land. To feel that I am communicating with hell through my body, floating on the primordial waters, and manage to touch the sky for an instant.

FINAL SILENCE

I hear his steps behind me. They break branches, make the fallen leaves rustle, tread on sacred ground. I turn and see his face. He is nearly at peace. He comes seeking his cure. As if his look has changed. He seems more relaxed. I am, myself, surprised at what I have been able to do. To annul myself so that he emerges. To convert myself into that voice guiding him in the darkness and allowing him to return whenever he needed to. I thought I would lose him several times. There were occasions when he was too close to staying on the other side. He could see the extent of his rage when, driven insane, he threw himself to the ground to kick, shout, writhe with fury. Of the ire he was sheltering within. Of the violence nourishing it. Of the pain that grew like a pustule, rotting him. It still terrifies me when I recall his shouts, his disproportionate weeping, that last occasion when I managed to make him speak to himself, enter a dialogue with himself, and he said things that, for a few seconds, split me asunder. I nearly lost control of that last session. We were at the Agua volcano's summit and he was on the point of throwing himself into the void. Such was his fury with himself. I only just managed to calm him down. I was able to bring him back from that altered state I had steered him into. From euphoria, he moved on to weeping. I remember him biting his fist, in a foetal position, sobbing until nightfall. He could not get through his ghost. I was near to ensuring that he did, but pushing him a little more would have meant losing him. He knew it. How close he had been; his failure to make it. I hope this time I complete my task and can finally put him in contact with himself and defeat that final silence interposed between him and his cure. Only time and the course of the exercise will tell. I get up and go over to meet him:

"As ever, López, you've arrived at the designated time."

I note that he has come ready in shorts and T-shirt. All that remains is to remove his shoes and watch in order to dive into the water. Moreover, he has a resolute expression. He hopes to approach the abyss that it represents and have no fear of launching himself to the other side. It's obvious he is ready to recover his innocence, or what remains of it.

I can see his expression is more cordial than ever. He seems comfortable. It has to be thus, because this therapy that's so strange is his invention, he feels in his element. I have to admit he's imaginative and that works in favour of the session being interesting and unique. But we're nearly at the end. In the last session I knew I was inside but grew scared of confronting my truths, passing through my ghost as he calls it. Defeating that final silence. But I could not. I felt diminished, useless, empty. I felt that, now, nothing could be done against the monster I myself had been and there was no longer any possibility of forgiveness. I sought to kill myself before forgiving myself. It was easier, but it wasn't possible. I had to tell myself what I had done. Tell myself this, and also tell myself that it was okay, that I had to accept the guilt and spew it out. Face up to my responsibility and settle accounts. I was unable to speak, leave that silence, say a word. I wasn't even able to put my hands in front of my face and say in a raised voice that with these hands I had killed defenceless people. It scared me so much. I wanted to leave myself as quickly as possible. But I went back. I don't even know how. I brought my hands to my face and wanted to say so many things but all that came out was that bitter and pained crying. I found myself saying "Mother, Mother, help me, lull me to sleep, I want to be in your lap and never have abandoned it, Mother; where are you because I can't find you, forgive me because now I myself cannot" and...I fell asleep. This time I'll have to do it. But it must not be my mother who forgives, but me. Me. There's Sandoval, waiting.

"As ever, Sandoval. And you always arrive early."

"Let's go to the canoe."

My feet sink into the sand and it's hard to walk. I advance slowly. As I have throughout this process. It still surprises me. I have always been curing victims; never, a victimiser. What is difficult is understanding that the pain is the same, the suffering of the victimiser is also deep, rooted, heart-rending. Something that has to be cured. It is a deeper darkness because violence is also his defence and when he feels threatened, he resorts to it. But when his mask is removed there also remains a destroyed individual, in rags, sensitive and wounded, one who needs to be rehabilitated. I have realised that, in the end, both human beings, victims and victimisers, suffer from the havoc caused by violence, they suffer and drag along their existence like a sentence. It's taken so much for me to become aware of this. I don't know if I have yet managed it fully.

Sandoval goes ahead and leaves the forest with a couple of strides.

"I hope it's not very far," I joke, trying to guess which of those rustic boats Sandoval would have rented to carry out the test.

"That one's ours," he says, pointing to one of the canoes that is no different from the others, just as simple and worn out.

"I hope it doesn't sink," I say in a jovial tone, hoping Sandoval laughs.

"I myself tried it this morning," I reply to López. I continue:

"My wife has been in town for several weeks. I arrived last Sunday, which is why I've been here a couple of days already. I took the opportunity to make all the arrangements. I don't think it's easy for the locals to rent you these boats. They fear strangers would not appreciate that the canoes are vessels of great importance to them."

"They must use them to fish with," I say, to make conversation. "It could not have been easy to convince someone to lend it to carry out a therapy session."

Sandoval laughs.

"Of course, I didn't go into details. I just said I wanted it to go on the lake and visit the Sunken City."

"Don't tell me you believe that nonsense," I say to him, because I'm sure Sandoval would have no time for what the locals make up to attract tourists. They say there's an ancient city submerged in the middle of the lake and charge those who want to see it – so as to take photos of some rocks covered in algae that can barely be seen in the water – a small fortune.

"No way," I answer López, who clearly assumes the legend is false.

"But it was much more believable for me to tell them that," I add. "That way there was no problem. Just a few banknotes, no questions asked."

They reach the canoe and Sandoval bends down to push it on to the lake. He takes a couple of steps in the water, wetting his shoes and ankles. The canoe is afloat. López stops for a moment to take off his shoes. Then, in an agile manoeuvre, he climbs over the side. Sandoval, who has now boarded, rows and the canoe begins to move away from the beach. The way they sit leaves them face to face. As Sandoval looks ahead, López can see what is being left behind. They glance at each other intermittently. Both go in silence. After several minutes, Sandoval stops rowing. They are in the middle of the lake. The waters are choppy and look deep. The wind worsens. The afternoon is falling away. They look at the volcanoes in the distance. The sky spreads out. The *xocomiles* start to appear, swirling away from the canoe.

"Well López, it's time to begin," I say as I start to remove my T-shirt and trousers, remaining just in trunks. The canoe continues on its course although at a much slower pace than before. It is left at the mercy of the swell.

"Okay Sandoval, let's begin," I say just before diving backwards into the water.

López falls in and splashes me. He remains completely submerged for a few seconds. He surfaces, takes a mouthful of air and smiles. It is noticeable how close he is getting to his objective. You could almost say he is happy. The expression on his face is nearly innocent.

"The water's cold!" I say, passing my hand over my eyes to see better.

I let out a juvenile howl while I take a couple of strokes towards the canoe where Sandoval is undressing. I can feel

FINAL SILENCE

the way the water supports my body and strokes my skin while I slip through it. It's fresh. It is like a caress that absorbs and envelops. It feels good, pleasurable. I put my whole head under. I submerge. I give a couple of dolphin kicks. I imagine I'm a whale and dive. I reach the surface and see the canoe several strokes away and Sandoval trying to take off his trousers but having difficulties. I submerge again. This time I imagine I'm a frog. I open my eyes beneath the water and see some enormous rocks, like temples, covered in algae. They are nearly within reach. I give a few more kicks and approach. A majestic silence invades me. I feel like part of the water and want to shout with joy for feeling this way. As if I were the first inhabitant of a sunken city. I'm going back to the surface to tell Sandoval of my discovery. Those stones I denied. To move faster, I put my feet on them, push and head back upwards with a thrust. I can see the canoe against the light. Almost like a plank floating. Sandoval's silhouette tying the pulls of his trunks, making that stupid knot. I do not manage to surface.

I see López coming from the depths. His face half sticks out of the water. But he remains submerged. He has an expression of happiness that I have never seen in anyone.

Something grabs my leg. It does not let go. I can't get out completely.

His hand appears at the surface. I see him waving it. He's greeting me. I return the greeting.

The waves cover me. Something pulls me down. I can't breathe.

I'm wrong. That face beneath the waves is one of anguish. Also the way he's waving his hand.

Something has entangled my leg. Sandoval, I'm tangled!
That hand is begging for help. López!
Sandoval, I can't breathe!
He has become entangled in the seaweed!
My shout doesn't come out, I just swallow water...
I'm very far.
I have no air.

Quick, I must row against the current!
Don't move away!
Now I can't see his hand!
The seaweed has...
López!
The orders that I should not...
Wait!
The forgiveness that...
Don't give in!
Mother?
You cannot die yet!
Are you still there?
Shall I dive in to save him?
Water surrounds me...
And if I can't make it?
water...
And if I do, will the canoe drift off and both of us die?
and...

    I row, but not towards López. I move further away. It is for the best. My professional work is done. I succeeded. I helped to cure Jorge Camacho, López, whoever. I put everything into it so you could forgive yourself. And you did.
    But I must tell you: I'm guilty. I can't forget. Sink with the stones. You don't matter to me any more.

    As much as he struggles with the seaweed, Camacho cannot untangle himself. He knows what awaits him. He has an impossible wish: to have preferred to die innocent. But it's too late now. He lets out a shout that becomes a gulp of water, his final silence. The horizon is lost within the swell. Clear blue. Sky blue. Emerald. The bubbles pass before his eyes that see ever less.